David S.E. Buchan

Essays on the Lives and Writings of Fletcher of Saltoun and the Poet Thomson

Biographical, critical, and political. With some pieces of Thomson's never before published

David S.E. Buchan

Essays on the Lives and Writings of Fletcher of Saltoun and the Poet Thomson
Biographical, critical, and political. With some pieces of Thomson's never before published

ISBN/EAN: 9783337012748

Printed in Europe, USA, Canada, Australia, Japan

Cover: Foto ©Raphael Reischuk / pixelio.de

More available books at **www.hansebooks.com**

Andrew Fletcher.

From an Authentick Portrait, in the Collection of the Earl of Buchan.

London Published Sep: 22. 1791 by J. Debrett.

ESSAYS

ON THE

LIVES AND WRITINGS

OF

FLETCHER OF SALTOUN

AND THE

POET THOMSON:

BIOGRAPHICAL, CRITICAL, AND POLITICAL.

With some Pieces of Thomson's never before published.

By *D. S. EARL OF BUCHAN.*

LONDON:

PRINTED FOR J. DEBRETT,
OPPOSITE BURLINGTON-HOUSE, PICCADILLY.

MDCCXCII.

7   *Thomson's*

CONTENTS.

An

A Hu-

N. B. THE Four last Articles were received by the Printer after all the others had gone to Press : otherwise the Earl of Buchan's Eulogy on Thomson, according to a natural Arrangement, would have been introduced in the Conclusion of this Volume.

INTRODUCTION.

ALTHOUGH I am fenfible that the very found and fight of the word LIBERTY has become difagreeable, if not terrible, to the fafhionable world in Britain; yet it is neceffary that I fhould introduce the Memoirs of Fletcher and Thomfon with reflections on the principles, manners, and temper, of the times and countries in which

B

they

they lived, and of thofe that preceded their appearance. It is my purpofe to treat this fub-ject very briefly.

It naturally divides itfelf into three parts; the Gothic, Puri-tanical, and Philofophical ages: under which three heads, with-out once mentioning the formi-dable and profcribed vocable, I fhall endeavour to make it clear and convincing to the meaneft and moft obdurate capacity, that political energy and fentiment were never wholly fuppreffed in my native country.

1ſt. Political energy and ſentiment eminently appeared in the Gothic, by which I literally denominate that age which was coeval with the formation of military governments on a feudal baſis, by the nations or people that over-ran Europe in ages far beyond the æra of genuine hiſtory, formed the ſtates of Greece and Italy, and afterwards in a more barbarous ſtate overſpred and overpowered the Roman empire, which had ſprung from the ſame original.

But the ſyſtem of Gothic go-

 vernment

vernment was permanent, and we have it accurately delineated by the mafterly hand of Tacitus, in his Treatife on the Situation, Cuftoms, and People of Germany.

In this æra, which is of immenfe duration, I obferve political energy and fentiment exemplified every where in the equal rights of the holders of the foil.

In countries and ages where lands were cultivated by flaves taken in war, or brought into bondage by conqueft, there could be no other citizens.

Trade and manufactures were not.

In such a posture of society sciences and arts could not exist.

The proprietors of the soil could not protect themselves without government; and government requires a prince either single or complex, elective or hereditary.

Governments were therefore formed variously, as contingency or necessity occasioned or required.---Scotland, the country to which my subject directs me, was planted and governed in this manner from the beginning.

The miferable natives who preceded the Goths or Scythians, were treated like the natives of North and South America by the Europeans; and, after fkulking and fcalping for ages in their faftneffes, muft have at laft yielded to neceffity or reafon in their obedience to the laws of the ftrongeft.

In England, after the dereliction of the Roman provinces by the legions, the enervated flaves of imperial Rome became

an

an eaſy prey to every hardy invader. *Veni, vidi, vici,* is a boaſt no way honourable or peculiar to Cæſar.

The Saxons and Danes, to go no farther, exemplified the motto with a vengeance; and I ſhall allow the baſtard of Normandy to have been a King William, and to have come over to ſave the miſerable Engliſh from Dane-gelt, ſlavery, and arbitrary power.

Great and big books have been written to ſhew that Engliſh law and liberty are as old

as

as the country. I diſlike big books, and leave Lord Lyttelton in poſſeſſion of the field.

If conſtitutions of government could be juſtly held to admit of no radical amendments, according to the political goſpel of Edmund, then the Gothic conſtitution was as perfect as poſſible.

But the rapid improvement of ſociety ſoon rendered it odious, unjuſt, and ridiculous.

To overthrow it, however, there was no people; for the king and the ſlaves were, in

fact,

fact, the only people, and the nobility was the prince.

The king, therefore, with the flaves, *affumed* the ftation of the people, and crufhed more or lefs in different ages and countries *the prince*, combined and compofed of the great proprietors of the foil.

This was accomplifhed by exciting and quelling impotent rebellions, by leaguing with the clergy, eftablifhing free towns and corporations, and by encouraging trade and navigation.

James I. King of Scots,

was

was far advanced in this plan when he was affaffinated by the Earl of Athol.   He had gone fo far to form a popular govern- ment by encouraging the leffer barons and the boroughs of Scotland, and by the attainder of the great earls, that he ufed to joke with his Queen (the great grand-daughter of Edward III.) faying, " My dear, I hope the day is not far diftant when I may have the pleafure of finding you in bed with all the nobility of Scotland!" a brave project for a patriot prince, and

worthy

worthy of a more fortunate iſſue!

A rich and powerful nobility (alias an oligarchy) muſt ſoon deſtroy the liberties of any people among whom they are ſuffered to domineer.

It is neceſſary to explain what the King of Scots meant by *all the nobility of Scotland.*

They were the Earls and Lords of Regality.

Scotland never knew ſuch a monſtrous order of men as Lords of Parliament.

The Earls had no right to ſit

in

in the Parliament but by their lands; but being chief magiſtrates and judges in their counties, with regal powers, theſe, with their territorial advantages ſpringing from the feudal ſyſtem, rendered them truly formidable both to the king and to the commonwealth.

James ſaw the advantages reaped in England by the crown, in conſequence of the formation of a peers houſe of parliament, and the power of calling up great commoners by writ of ſummons to that houſe of parliament, and

wiſhed

wished to adopt so crafty an example.

On the trial of Murdoch, Duke of Albany, he established a precedent for what were called Barons of Baron-rent, to be called Lords and Nobles, and to sit with precedence in the parliament by royal charter of lands, erecting estates into earldoms or baronies, unconnected with the ancient earldoms or county palatines of the kingdom; and, then, by the election of certain members of parliament, for preparing the

laws

laws or acts, who were called the Lords of the Articles, chosen from the earls, barons of baron-rent, and the great officers of the state, he contrived to quash or prevent motions that were adverse to the interest of the crown*.

I blush to repeat the A B C of the political history of Britain; but as I have not met with a short essence of it in any of our modern novels, I hope I may be excused, at least, by ladies and gentlemen who seldom turn over unwieldy vo-

* See Burnet's History of his Own Times.

lumes.

lumes. Thus the creation of a tiers etat, or, of the weight of the people in the political balance, as is well obferved in Captain Newte's admirable Tour in Scotland, was not the work of patriots, but of kings. In Sir William Wallace, the *Tell* of Scotland, we have a precious unique in the Gothic age of Scottifh political energy and fentiment; and had Scotland belonged by hereditary claims to England or France, he would probably have engaged his countrymen to have formed a republic like the Swifs.

He

He was envied and hated by the earls and great barons of Scotland; and by *their* treachery he fell a martyr to the independency and liberties of his country. It is in vain to fearch for the moral and rational principles of government in the military Gothic age: in thofe wretched times men had no civic union, no proper interchange of political fentiment. Fixed, or rather chained as they were to the foil of their mafters, the people were without collifion of fentiment; had no organized focieties for

the

the contemplation of common interests; no high roads, no posts, no printing-presses! What is man in such a situation, but the machine of regal or princely ambition and luxury!

II. I come now to consider the puritanical age of political energy and sentiment. Nothing could have been more fortunate for mankind, than the destruction of the degraded Greek empire by the Turks, so soon after the dissemination of the doctrines of Wickliffe, and the reformers of the church of Rome.

It

It gave Europe philoſophers, and teachers, and men of learning, Greek, and ſenſe, and ſpirit.

Human genius and ſentiment are always moſt agreeably excited by the contemplation of misfortunes. We naturally attach ourſelves to the ſide of the loſer of a conteſt. The ſtruggles for liberty in Greece and Italy, recorded ſo eloquently by the Greek and Roman claſſics, imbued the minds of youth, and excited the feelings of the aged with the ardour of political ſentiment. The people then began

to

to know truly what it is to be a member of a free commonwealth, to be a citizen: delightful name! beſt of inheritances, beſt of rights, not to be ſurrendered, but with the life that accompanies it! With theſe ſublime and heart-engaging affections, the ſtudy of the Scriptures of Moſes and the Evangeliſts in the living languages of Europe, and the conſolation of free agency in the choice of religious opinions, remarkably contributed to the creation of new political energy among all ranks

of

of men, but particularly among the middling and lower claſſes of the people, who by religious controverſy were made, as it were, artificial members of ſociety, and felt the inexpreſſible and captivating delight of thinking and acting for themſelves, and of touching and affecting general ſociety.—The clergy, irritated to madneſs by the diſſolution of their magic ſuperſti-tion, and looking forward to the total deſtruction of their profit-able fable of the church, perſecuted the thinking and reform-

ing

ing people; and this laid the foundation of that perception of religious liberty, which immediately connected itself with political liberty in Scotland so early as the reign of James V. and in England towards the end of the reign of Queen Elizabeth.

Buchanan arose in Scotland like the morning star, to announce the approach of philosophical day.

He was the father of whiggery *as a system* in Britain, if not in Europe; the Lord Bacon or Newton of political science and

senti-

sentiment, by far the greatest man of his age, as Napier was of his country, in invention: in as much as political science is above all others in real importance, with respect to which we may fairly set down every other with an adject of a " haud simile aut secundum." To women, some how or other, we have been indebted from the beginning for fortunate revolutions, saving in the case of Lady Adam, and even that is not carbonified by the strictest theologians.

To the beauty, gaiety, and

im-

imprudence of Mary Stuart, the daughter of James V. we are indebted for the prefent ftate of Britain, fuch as it is. Had Mary been prudent, Scotland might have become a Popifh monarchy. England at beft would have been under its old monarchy (with proper addrefs), under the Stuarts; and we fhould not have had occafion to deprecate Gallic freedom with the monftrous infanity of modern Englifhmen; but to deplore the want of it.

It were needlefs and fuperfluous for me in this fketch to

deli-

delineate the minute progrefs of puritanical patriotifm, from the depofition of Mary Queen of Scots, to that of her great grand-fon James the Seventh of Scotland, and Second of England.

In Scotland, even down to the period of the union of the kingdoms and parliaments, the people had no nerves for feeling political fentiment, fave through the medium of religion or fuperftition.

Give Sawney his Sunday's minifter to his liking, and he cared not who were minifters of of ftate. Even during the long paper as well as cartridge war in the laft century, we hear and fee little in their acts or writings that favoured in the leaft of moral or political liberty. Every thing fmelt of the fcarlet lady of Rome. There were Scottifh Hampdens, but no Sidneys. Buchanan and Fletcher alone were elevated above the ages in which they lived, and fhed a luftre towards thofe that were to fucceed, which will continue to fhine more and more unto the perfect day. I glory in being the attire-

man

man of the characters of such *figurative princes;* and rejoice to think that even in that humble connection my name may be handed down to diftant pofte-rity! My anceftor Marr was a favourite pupil of Buchanan's, imbibed his fcience and princi-ples, and handed them down to the race of the Stuart Erfkines. I glory alfo, therefore, in pay-ing this family tribute to that glorious pedagogue.

III. I proceed now with plea-fure to the age of philofophical politics, which Thomfon, my

favourite

favourite bard, and the bard of liberty, ſaw before his death, like another prophet from Piſgah, ſaw and rejoiced !

The act of parliament which put an end to the heretable juriſdictions in Scotland, together with the wiſe and prudent adminiſtration of Archibald Duke of Argyl, and Lord Milton, gave Scotland a free avenue to political and civil exertion: the land was fallow, and cultivated by honeſt and active huſbandmen, it preſently bore abundant harveſts. It would be invidious in

my

my own times to felect names for enumeration and eulogy. They whom I have formerly named and celebrated will *not* be faved from oblivion by my feeble efforts. They would have lived without my encomium. Yet I arrogate to myfelf fome degree of praife that I was taught, and that I learnt how to difcriminate tinfel from gold. Hume, and Napier, and Fletcher, and Buchanan, and Thomfon, will live for ever. Can I enough regret that Hume was a tory, and a foolifh enthufiaft in fcepticifm?

Yet

Yet I will not attempt to touch his immortality; *my* shafts would but rebound from *his* seven-fold shield. To the divine influence of the *printing-press* is the world indebted for the reign of philosophy; and to philosophy it owes the principles of legislation.

It is with infinite regret that I cannot pretend to produce from Scotland, during this halcyon reign of philosophy, any great character since the death of Fletcher; for Thomson was a retired man, and quite out of the walk of political eminence.

What

What could be expected from a country, where the hereditary members of parliament were impotent, and fearfully queftioned each other on the diffolution of a parliament, who were named to be of the fixteen reprefentatives of the nobility of the country and nation? I beheld this infamous degradation of gentlemen, for I will not fpeak of noblemen, with difguft. I called upon the electors to roufe from their baneful lethargy; and they thought I was about to raife a third rebellion. Yet I perfevered.

vered. By and by they began to leap the fold: they found their account in it; and they also perfevered. But I will fay no more about *them*: liberty, and Buchanan, and Fletcher, and Thomfon, are better themes, or at leaft better fuited to my humble genius.

I ftop rather to enquire concerning the comparative ftate of Britain, in this philofophical age of political fentiment, with France and other countries, that have had inferior advantages.

Who but a clerk of the treafury,

fury, or a lord of the king's bed-chamber, can contemplate this parallel without regret?

It was in the laſt war of George II. that Great Britain laid herſelf under the neceſſity of defending her wide-extended dominion; and of aſſerting her claim to be the firſt nation upon earth. The conteſt was bloody and expenſive, but the end was glorious—The enemy proſtrate and breathleſs, empire extended, honour maintained, peace eſtab-liſhed, and, like the ſun riſing after a ſtorm, a young and na-

tive

tive monarch holding the fceptre, and afcending the throne,
amidft the acclamations of the
freeft and happieft people on the
globe.

Thefe acclamations are heard
no more. A fyftem of corruption, eftablifhed and digefted
early in this reign *by a baneful
ariftocracy*, has pervaded every
rank and order of men, till the
fpirit of the conftitution has
fled, and left only the *caput
mortuum* behind. The forms of
our government have out-lafted
the ends for which they were

D inſtiinftituted, and have become a mere mockery of the people for whofe benefit they fhould operate.

The prophecy of Montef-quieu is fulfilled; and nothing can fave the country but the fulfilment of the prophecy of Franklin. What that prophecy was, what this prophecy is, I leave to the curious to learn. What I have written, I have written: futurity will determine the truth of my own particular predictions, and whether I am to be remembered as a captious Cynic,

Cynic, or a wife and Pythonic politician.

To conclude: As I think it unneceffary to delineate the fpirit of the times in Europe with refpect to government, fo I think it to be indifpenfably required at my hands, that I fhould, with refpect to Scotland, deprecate the refufal of a militia to my country, the neceffity for which was fo eloquently fet forth by my favourite Fletcher.

That I fhould mark with my blackeft coal the game licence act, which is an infidious and

dan-

dangerous difarming of the commons.

That I fhould exprefs my utter deteftation and abhorrence of the conduct of a firft minifter, who calling himfelf the minifter of the crown, with a treafonable audacity fhould dare to advife the diffolution of a parliament, againft the fenfe of a houfe of commons, the only legal organ of the voice of the people, let that houfe be ever fo ill conftructed, and demand ever fo much reformation.

That

That I ſhould loudly pro-
teſt, that a parliament ought to
be allowed to die a natural
death. And,

That if a parliament, contem-
plating the foreboding, the ominous imperfections of the conſtitution, ſhould on its death-
bed provide for a remedy by the
equalization of the repreſenta-
tion of the people, it would
prevent the dangerous concuſ-
ſion which muſt undoubtedly
ariſe, *and that quickly*, from
their political franchiſes being
brought to the level of ſur-

 round-

rounding nations with a violent jerk. Let us not (said my admirable preceptor and friend, Adam Smith, author of the Essay on the Wealth of Nations) rashly believe that Great Britain is capable of supporting any burden.

Let us consider what hold we have *now* of the two Indies, of Canada, and our other lucrative dependencies. A blow may be struck, a blow will be struck, that shall reach the vitals of public credit, and it is an event which nothing but

poli-

political infanity can induce public minifters not to provide againft. But no provifion can be made againft this event, except that which has been pointed out by the finger of the genius of Britain's welfare.

I will not offer incenfe to the living, but to the dead: I infcribe this and the following fheets to the memory of Sir GEORGE SAVILE, of Rufford Hall, Member of Parliament for the County of York.

THE

LIFE

OF

ANDREW FLETCHER

OF SALTOUN.

By D. S. EARL of BUCHAN.

Among innumerable falfe, unmov'd,
Unfhaken, unfeduc'd, unterrify'd,
Nor number, nor example with him wrought
To fwerve from truth, or change his conftant mind,
Though fingle.

PARADISE LOST, b. v.

THE
LIFE
OF
ANDREW FLETCHER
OF SALTOUN.

WHEN I did myself the honour, with the affiftance of the learned profeffor Minto, to offer to the public an account of the life, writings, and difcoveries of the inventor of the logarithms, I pledged myfelf to attempt the biography of Fletcher of Saltoun, and of John Law of Lauriefton: but when I fet myfelf to the work, I found it much more difficult than I had imagined.

I confefs

I confefs that I am ambitious of permanent reputation, and loath to hazard even the little I may have obtained in promoting that of others, by obtruding on the world what might be brought forward by men of fuperior abilities. But, feveral years having elapfed without my having any profpect of being anticipated, I have yielded to the impulfe of my efteem for the character of Fletcher.

I am afraid, however, that this monument which I endeavour to raife to the memory of my patriotic countryman may induce me to write too freely upon the fubjects which excited my defire to perpetuate his name: but whether I may pleafe or offend the prefent little world of the day, when I decently exprefs the feelings of my heart, or the refult of my reflections, it will give me little concern.

I am

I am the creature of a day, but not the creature of the times.

In politics I would be a Diogenes; and if patronifed by the great Alexander of modern politics, whoever may affect that character, I fhould defire him, as my only requeft, that he would ftand out of my light, that I might behold the beautiful fabric of a free conftitution, undazzled by the fplendour of power, and unintoxicated by the opinion of the people.

Andrew Fletcher of Saltoun was the fon of Sir Robert Fletcher of Saltoun and Innerpeffer, by Catharine Bruce, daughter of Sir Henry Bruce of Clackmannan.   By his paternal defcent he was of a family truly honourable, and by his maternal, of the royal race of Bruce; the patriarch of the family of Clackmannan having been the third fon of Robert de Bruce, lord of Annandale, grandfather of

Robert

Robert de Bruce, king of the Scots. His father was the fifth in lineal defcent from Sir Bernard Fletcher of the county of York *. He married Catharine Bruce in the year 1651; and his eldeft fon Andrew, the fubject of my enquiry, was born in the year 1653 †.

When he had the misfortune to lofe his father, he was but in his early youth, and was deftined by his father, on his death-bed, to the care of Dr. Burnet, rector of the parifh of Saltoun, afterwards bifhop of Salifbury, well known

---

* Sir Robert's father Andrew was one of the fenators of the College of Juftice in Scotland, by the ftyle of Lord Innerpefter. He was one of thofe feven truly magnanimous Scots who, with David Lord Cardrofs, protefted againft the delivery of King Charles I. at Newcaftle, to the Englifh Parliament. He died 1650.—MS. hift. of the family in my poffeffion.

† MS. hift. ut fupra.

by

by his political zeal and interefting writings. From Burnet he received, as might have been expected, a very pious and learned education, and was ftrongly imbued with erudition and the principles of a free government, which were congenial to the family of Fletcher, and efpoufed by his mother, and by thofe who had, with her, the charge of his nurture *.

When he had completed his courfe of elementary ftudies in Scotland, under the care of his excellent preceptor, he was fent to travel on the continent.

He was from his infancy of a very fiery and uncontroulable temper; but his difpofitions were noble and generous †.

* MS. hift. ut fupra.

† MS. hift. ut fupra; from which, where not diftinguifhed by other reference, I fhall draw all my authorities.

He

He became firſt known as a public ſpeaker and a man of political energy, being commiſſioner in the Scotch parliament for the ſhire of Eaſt Lothian, when the Duke of York was lord commiſſioner, connecting himſelf with the Earl of Argyll in oppoſition to the Duke of Lauderdale's adminiſtration, and the arbitrary deſigns of the court, which obliged him to retire firſt into England to conſult with Dr. Burnet, and afterwards, by his advice, into Holland. He was ſummoned to appear before the Lords of the Council at Edinburgh, which he not thinking it prudent for him to do, he was outlawed, and his eſtate confiſcated.

In the year 1683 he, with Robert Baillie of Jerviſwood, came into England in order to concert meaſures with the friends of freedom in that country; and

they,

they, I believe, were the only Scotchmen who were admitted into the fecrets of Lord Ruffel's Council of Six. They were likewife the only perfons in whom the Earl of Argyll confided in Holland the common meafures of the two countries, which were then concerted with much fecrecy and danger, for the recovery of the conftitution and liberties of the Britifh kingdoms.

Fletcher managed his part of the negociation with fo much addrefs and prudence, that Adminiftration, though in no refpect delicate as to the means of reaching the objects of their jealoufy or refentment, could find no pretext for feizing him, nor could they fix upon him any of the articles of impeachment for which Mr. Baillie of Jervifwood was condemned and fuffered capital punifhment. Mr.

E

Baillie

Baillie was offered his pardon on condition of impeaching his friend Fletcher; but he perfifted to the gallows in rejecting the propofal with indignation.   O noble, excellent, and truly worthy Scot! May your defcendants and your countrymen ever remember and imitate your example!

On Fletcher's return to the continent, finding no profpect of his fafe return to Britain, he dedicated his leifure to foreign travel, and to the ftudy of public law and politics; during which period of his life I have fruitlefsly fought for letters that might not only have traced him in his various fituations, but furnifhed agreeable and ufeful materials for his biography.

In the beginning of the year 1685 Fletcher came to the Hague, to affift at the deliberations of the exiles from Britain, and particularly with thofe of his

own

own country, with a view to promote the caufe of oppofition to the arbitrary meafures of James II : but it does not appear that he poffeffed much of the confidence of the party. He was unaccommodating, and ran extravagantly on the project of fetting up a commonwealth in Scotland, or at leaft a monarchy fo limited as hardly to bear any refemblance to a kingdom. His foul was fired with the recollection of the great fpirits that had been raifed by the Greek republics, and, like all men of great abilities, he wifhed for that ftate of things which might mark the fuperiority of his own talents, and give full exercife to his popular powers. Argyll's expedition concerted at that time with Monmouth and the party was the moft inviting to Fletcher ; but being diffatisfied with the plan of operations, and

E 2

his

his countrymen, who enjoyed Monmouth's confidence, he went with the Duke, who was the dupe of the ambitious and crafty Prince of Orange *.

Burnet,

* The ambitious and crafty Prince of Orange.] It is with reluctance that I affix such epithets to a prince who feems to be, as it were, the idol of whigs, who, in hyperbolifing the immortal memory of Old Glorious, feem to forget that he was a man, and a politician. My grandfather and great-grandfather came over with him at the Revolution; and I know that I am not without partiality to a character connected with the eftablifhment of what we call the Conftitution of the country, and with the illuftration of my own family: but I cannot be blind to his faults, nor do I think it would be conducive to the eftablifhment of a real conftitution of freedom in the Britifh nation, that fuch blindnefs fhould continue among the people who wifh to arrange themfelves under the banners of Britifh liberty. That he was ambitious in the difagreeable appli-

cation

Burnet, in the Hiftory of his Own

Times, informs us that Fletcher had told

him,

cation of that epithet appears from his lulling the flumbers of royal fecurity in England, when he was fanning the flames of infurrection againft his father-in-law in Holland; from his encouraging the mad project of Monmouth to get him out of the way to the throne, while he was giving good advice to James that the invafion might be defeated. That he was craftily ambitious, appears not only from this double plot, but from his forcing his way to the throne, inftead of accepting the regency, by intimidating the chiefs who had invited him over, with a threat of returning to Holland, and leaving them in the hands of an enraged bigoted monarch. That he was ambitious, crafty, and machiavelian, appears from his having given inftructions *to take care* of King James, if he fhould remain at Rochefter, and not be difpofed to leave the kingdom. Of the wretched device to fhake the confidence of the people with refpect to the Queen's pregnancy, and the Prince of Wales's birth, I fhall fay nothing. It

him, that Monmouth, though a weak young man, was fenfible of the imprudence of his adventure, and hefitated till he was urged by the party, moft·of whom were certainly in concert with the Prince of Orange, and confidered him as the only probable inftrument for dethron-

is the difgrace of the party, and ought to be buried, if poffible, in oblivion. It is a dangerous as well as a wicked thing for a prince to take fuch methods of infuring fuccefs, as William himfelf afterwards found, by the intrigues of the Princefs Sophia to turn him out: the proofs of which intrigues King William tied up together in a bundle, which was found in his cabinet. They were feen in Lord Rochford's hands while fecretary of ftate, were afterwards in other hands that need not be mentioned, and were probably treated as heretics were formerly, and as republicans are now wifhed to be by fome other kings. The bundle was docketted by William's own hand—" *Letters of the Princefs Sophia to turn me out.*"

ing

ing the king, and fupplanting William in his views, if the attempt were delayed till the Englifh nation fhould become defperate enough to overlook the doubts that Charles II. had confirmed by his declaration in council of the legitimacy of the Duke of Monmouth*. So well was this plot laid, that few of the party in Holland joined in thefe expeditions, but waited either in or out of the fecret, till they fhould fee the effects of the explofion that was to bury poor Monmouth under its

* Thofe men urged him on to war and danger, by an appeal to his perfonal courage. They wifhed in this manner to remove a dangerous rival out of the way of the prince's ambition; well-knowing that if the people of England fhould become defperate, they might be induced to overlook the doubts of Monmouth's legitimacy, which had been confirmed by the public declaration of Charles II.

E 4

ruins.

ruins. But Fletcher of Saltoun had neither coolness nor sufficient political subtlety to conduct himself with a view to his own private emolument. Fired by the hopes of a revolution that, from the insignificancy of Monmouth, and the circumstances of his birth, might produce a constitution of government in which his republican talents might have full scope, he at first fell in warmly with the scheme of Monmouth's landing; but afterwards, suspecting probably the intrigue of the Prince of Orange, he wished it to be laid aside. He told Bishop Burnet (which supports this conjecture), that Monmouth was pushed on to it against his own sense and reason, and was picqued upon the point of honour in hazarding his person with his friends. Monmouth landed at Lime in Dorsetshire. Soon after their landing,

Lord

Lord Grey was sent with a small party to disperse a few of the militia, and ran for it; but his men stood, and the militia retreated. Lord Grey brought back a false report, which was soon contradicted by the men, whom their leader had abandoned, coming back to quarters in good order. The unfortunate Duke of Monmouth was struck with this (says Burnet), when he found that the person on whom he depended most, and for whom he designed the command of the cavalry, had already made himself infamous by his cowardice. He intended to join Fletcher with him in that command *: but Fletcher having been sent out on another party, engaged in a scuffle, in which he had the misfortune to kill the mayor of

* Burnet.

Lynn

Lynn againſt the laws of war, in the ſud-
den heat of paſſion, on account of con-
tumelious language uſed to him by the
mayor, on reclaiming a horſe of his that
had been impreſſed by Fletcher's party.
This unguarded, unſoldierly, and unjuſti-
fiable act of violence, muſt have rendered
his future ſervices on the expedition of
little conſideration to Monmouth; but it
was not the cauſe of his leaving the little
army. The account given by Fletcher
himſelf of his general conduct at this
time to the late Earl Marſhall of Scotland,
was, that he had been induced to join the
Duke of Monmouth, on the principles of
the Duke's manifeſtoes in England and
Scotland, particularly by the laws pro-
miſed for the permanent ſecurity of civil
and political liberty, and of the proteſtant
religion, and the calling of a general con-

greſs

grefs of delegates from the people at large, to form a free conftitution of government, and not to pretend to the throne upon any claim, except the free choice of the reprefentatives of the people. That, when Monmouth was proclaimed king at Taunton, he faw his deception, and refolved to proceed no farther in his engagements, which he confidered from that moment as treafon againft the juft rights of the nation, and treachery on the part of Monmouth. That, finding himfelf therefore no longer capable of being ufeful, he left Taunton, and embarked on board a veffel for Spain. That foon after his landing he was committed to prifon; and, on the application of the Englifh minifter at Madrid, he was ordered to be delivered up, and tranfmitted to London in a Spanifh veffel, which was named for that purpofe.

That

That one morning, as he was looking pen-
fively through the bar of his dungeon, he
was accosted by a venerable person, who
made sign to speak to him. Fletcher, looking if any passage could be found for his
escape, discovered a door open, at which he
was met by his deliverer, with whom he
passed unmolested through three guards
of soldiers, who were fast asleep; and,
without being permitted to return thanks
to his guide, he prosecuted his escape
with the aid of a person who seemed to
have been sent for that purpose, concerning whom he never could obtain any in-
formation. That disguised he proceeded
in safety through Spain, where, when he
found himself out of all apparent danger,
he lingered, and amused himself with the
view of the country, and with study in
the conventual libraries; and having pri-

vately

vately obtained credit by bills upon Amsterdam, he bought many rare and curious books, fome of which are preferved in the library at Saltoun, in the county of Haddinton. That he had made feveral very narrow efcapes of being detected and feized in the courfe of his peregrinations through Spain, particularly in the neighbourhood of a town (the name of which Lord Marfhall had forgotten), where he intended to have paffed the night; but in the fkirts of a wood a few miles diftant from thence, upon entering a road to the right, he was warned by a woman of a very refpectable appearance, to take the left-hand road, as there would be danger in the other direction. Upon his arrival he found the citizens alarmed by the news of a robbery and murder on the road againft which he had been cautioned. Some time after this

efcape,

escape, Fletcher's active genius led him to serve as a volunteer in the Hungarian war *, where he distinguished himself by his gallantry and military talents. But the glory which he might have acquired in arms, had he served long enough to have obtained a command, he cheerfully sacrificed to the safety of his country.

Persuaded that the liberties of Britain, if not of all Europe, hung upon the issue of the design then in contemplation at the Hague for a revolution in England, and having learned that it had already attained a considerable degree of maturity, he hastened to Holland, and joined himself to the groupe of his countrymen who were attached to the interests of the Prince of Orange, most of whom were refugees from England or Scotland. Lord Stair,

* MS. ut supra.

Lord

Lord Melville, Sir Patrick Hume of Polwarth, Lord Cardrofs, Sir Robert Steuart of Coltnefs, Dr. Burnet, Mr. James Stuart, afterwards lord advocate of Scotland, and Mr. Cunningham, the editor of Horace, and author of a Latin Hiftory of Great Britain, which has been lately tranflated by Dr. W. Thomfon, continuator of principal Watfon's Hiftory of Spain, and author of feveral Philofophical Romances, &c. &c. and publifhed by Dr. Hollingberry, one of the prefent king's chaplains, were the Scots with whom he was in the greateft habits of intimacy *. With thefe gentlemen Fletcher

cher

---

* Though I hold in fovereign contempt the infignificance of modern anecdote, I fhall fet down in this place fome particulars relating to thefe men, that are characteriftic of their times and hiftories, that may not be unacceptable to the public. Sir Patrick Hume of Polwarth, grandfather of the prefent

fent

cher affociated; but his political principles were too high and refined, and his fenti-

ments

fent Earl of Marchmont, from his firft appearance in the Scotch parliament, in the year 1665, as member for the county of Berwick, had diftinguifhed himfelf by a noble zeal for the liberties of his country. He was the ableft man of the party in oppofition to the adminiftration of the worthlefs Lauderdale; and in the year 1675, when, according to the defpotic fyftem of that fcandalous engine of the court, the Scotch privy council, the houfes of perfons difagreeable to adminiftration were made barracks of for the troops, he had the fpirit to bring a complaint into the courts of juftice with refpect to the garrifoning the houfe of Blanfe in Berwickfhire; for the exercife of which right he was brought before the privy council, who declared him incapable of all public truft, committing him prifoner to the common tolbooth or jail of Edinburgh, where he underwent a long and tedious imprifonment, from whence, upon petition on account of ficknefs, he was conveyed to the caftle of Dunbarton, and afterwards to Stirling

caftle,

ments were too Roman, or rather, as I may now fay, too Gallic, and too much in

caftle, where he remained fome years. When liberated, he retired into England, where being in ftrict habits of friendfhip with the friends of liberty, and particularly with Lord Ruffel, he found it neceffary for him to go abroad on the breaking out of the Rye-houfe plot, and lived fome time at Geneva, from whence he went to the Hague, to concert with his fellow-fufferers the meafures that were followed by the expeditions of Monmouth and Argyll, with the latter of whom he came over, and narrowly efcaped being taken after the defeat of Argyll's forces, taking fhelter and lying in concealment in the houfe of the Laird of Langfhaw, and afterwards in the aifle of the church of Polwarth, the burial-place of his family. All his food was brought to him in the night time by his eldeft daughter, then only twelve years old. This place of concealment having been difcovered, a party was fent to apprehend him. As the foldiers paffed near a gentle-

F

man's

in the odour of philofophical politics, to
accept of the privilege granted by James

                                        the

man's houfe in the neighbourhood, who was friendly,
to Sir Patrick, and to liberty, they were invited by
him, who knew their errand, to caroufe on his ale,
and beft cheer; while he, aware of the danger of
writing, immediately fent a feather inclofed in a
bit of paper, as a fymbol of flight, to Sir Patrick in
the aifle at Polwarth; who, prefently interpreting the
figure, took horfe, and fortunately efcaped and fled
into Holland, where he remained under the feigned
name of Brown, till he came over with the Prince
of Orange at the Revolution.

Sir Patrick was born on the 13th of January
1641; appointed lord chancellor of Scotland May
2d, 1696; lord high commiffioner, or lord lieutenant
of Scotland, 1702. He died at Berwick on the 1ft
of Auguft 1724, in the 84th year of his age, highly
refpected for his attachment to the liberties of his
country, for his virtue, religion, and learning. His
fon and heir Alexander, Earl of Marchmont, after

                                        a feries

the Second's act of indemnity to return
to his country and eftate, when under the
dominion

a feries of political fituations, not coming as one
does now-a-days from being a fchool-boy to be a
prime minifter, was our ambaffador at the congrefs
of Cambray in the year 1721; and his fon Hugh,
now Earl of Marchmont, made a brilliant figure in
the Houfe of Commons in oppofition to the corrupt
adminiftration of Sir Robert Walpole, and was afterwards an ufeful member of the Houfe of Peers, yet
moft of all diftinguifhed by his learning, and by
having been the friend of Pope, Swift, Atterbury, and
Arbuthnot. Party politics in England cannot fecure
permanent fame; and I rejoice to think that my old
good friend, the friend of my father and grandfather, has fecured his immortality by literature.

In his philofophic retreat at Hemel Hempfted, he
may perhaps deign to be flattered with my hereditary regard.

Henry Lord Cardrofs, the fon of David Lord
Cardrofs of Dryburgh, &c. who protefted againft

he

dominion of difguifed defpotifm, fancti-
fied by a venal parliament: fo that

when

the delivering up of King Charles I. at Newcaftle,
had been trained, in the manner of his family, in
the exalted principles of religion, liberty, and learning; and early joined himfelf to the oppofers of the
Duke of Lauderdale's adminiftration. For his lady's
hearing her own chaplain preach in her own houfe,
he was fined in five thoufand pounds, of which he
paid a thoufand; and, after many months attendance
at court for procuring a difcharge of the overplus of
his fine, was finally imprifoned in the caftle of Edinburgh, where he continued four years; while his
houfe of Cardrofs in Perthfhire, immediately after
it had been repaired, and furnifhed at a great expence, was garrifoned to his great lofs and vexation.
And in June 1679, the king's forces, in their march to
the weft (the day before the Duke of Buccleugh came
to them), wheeled and went about two miles out of
the road, that they might quarter on Lord Cardrofs's
eftates of Kirkhall and Uphall, in Weft Lothian.,

After-

when Argyll, Sutherland, Melville, and others had recovered their inheritances

in

Afterwards, having obtained his liberation, he went to North America, and eftablifhed a colony in Carolina, which was deftroyed by the Spaniards. He returned, broken but not difpirited by misfortunes, to Europe, and attached himfelf to the friends of liberty in Holland. He raifed a regiment of dragoons, on the Revolution, and was an ufeful commander under M'Kay in Scotland, in fubduing the remains of oppofition there to the new government; but died of the effects of his fufferings, in the year 1693, in the 43d year of his age.——Concerning Sir Robert Steuart of Coltnefs, there is an anecdote fo hiftorically curious, that I cannot pafs him over without notice, though he was a perfon of no extraordinary eminence. In the end of the year 1686, when the bufinefs of the Teft was in agitation, William Penn was employed at the court of the Prince of Orange, to reconcile the Stadtholder to the views of his father-in-law. Penn became acquainted with moft

of

in the year 1686, he chose rather to remain in exile than to accept of liberty

as

of the Scotch fugitives, and, among the rest, with Sir Robert Steuart, and his brother James, who wrote the famous Answer to Fagel's Memorial, and will be mentioned more particularly hereafter: and finding that the violence of their zeal reached little farther than the enjoyment of their religious liberty, on his return to London he advised the measure of an indemnity and recal to the persecuted Presbyterians, who had not been engaged in treasonable acts of opposition to the civil government. Sir Thomas availed himself of this indemnity to return to his own country; but found his estate and only means of subsistence in the possession of the Earl of Arran, afterwards Duke of Hamilton. Soon after his coming to London he met Penn, who congratulated him on his being just about to feel experimentally the pleasure so beautifully expressed by Horace, of the " Mihi me reddentis agelli." Coltness sighed, and said, " Ah, Mr. Penn! Arran has got

my

as a royal favour!   Yet Alexander Cunningham, the hiftorian, though a Whig

and

my eftate, and I fear my fituation is about to be now
worfe than ever."   "What do you fay, Gofpel?" (a
name Coltnefs had got at the Hague :) "You furprife
and grieve me exceedingly.   Come to my houfe to-
morrow, and I will fet matters to rights for thee."

Penn went immediately to Arran.   "What is this,
friend James," faid he to him, "that I hear of thee?
Thou haft taken poffeffion of Coltnefs's eftate; thou
knoweft that it is not thine."   "That eftate," replied
Arran, "I paid a great price for.   I received no
other reward for my expenfive and troublefome em-
baffy in France except this eftate; and I am certainly much out of pocket by the bargain."

"All very well, friend James," faid the Quaker;
"but of this affure thyfelf, that if thou doft not give
me this moment an order on thy chamberlain for
two hundred pounds to Coltnefs, to carry him down
to his native country, and a hundred a year to fub-
fift on till matters are adjufted, I will make it as

many

and friend of Fletcher, mentions this conduct of Fletcher's as extravagant. It was reserved for this age of wonders to exhibit the true principles of political fentiment, unconnected with fuperftition and perfonal attachment to kings or to parties.

Fletcher made a manly, noble appear-

many thoufands out of thy way with the king." Arran inftantly complied, and Penn fent for Sir Robert, and gave him the fecurity. After the Revolution, Sir Thomas, with the reft, had full reftitution of his eftate, and Arran was obliged to account for all the rents he had received; againft which this payment only was allowed to be ftated.—This authentic particular I received from my illuftrious uncle, the late Sir James Steuart Denham, father of the prefent worthy member for Clydefdale. It ftrongly marks the keennefs of King James to facilitate his foolifh meafures in favour of his religion and arbitrary power.

ance

ance in that convention which met in Scotland, after the Revolution, for the settlement of the new government. In Scotland the rights and liberties of the people had been determined and fixed by multiplied inftances of changing the order of fucceffion, and attainting their fovereigns for treafon againft the rights of the people: and it is to Scotland and a Scotchman that the world is indebted for the eftablifhment of the philofophical and logical principles of a free conftitution both in theory and practice. George Buchanan, the greateft man of his age, as well as country, eftablifhed, by irrefragable arguments, in his treatife or dialogue concerning the rights of the people of Scotland, the rights of all mankind; was the father of whiggery, and, what is much grander, the father of that fyftem which

which will one day verify the prophecies of the Chriftian Scriptures, to the abafe-ment of kings, and the deftruction of prieftcraft.

Raymond de Sebonde in France, the friend of Montaigne, adopted the prin-ciples of Buchanan in his Lettre fur la Ser-vitude Volontaire, a beautiful little piece publifhed by his friend, which being uni-verfally read with the Effays of Mon-taigne, kept up the facred fire of freedom in France, in the midft of folly and defpo-tifm, till the progrefs of commerce, print-ing, philofophy, and literature opened the eyes of Frenchmen every where to difcover that they were men, and ought to be citizens; that men were not born with *gold chains* about their necks, with ftars upon their breafts, or coronets upon their heads; that it is of the nature of kings

as

as hitherto conftituted, to confider their interefts as feparate from their nations, and to watch continually like wolves or foxes for their prey, in order to deftroy the citizens committed to their charge; that it is neceffary, therefore, that they fhould have only the power of obeying the laws made by the people, with that of doing good; but that the power of doing mifchief, either by prerogative or *influence*, ought to be taken away. Thefe were the principles of Fletcher, principles that feemed extravagant, difloyal, and impracticable in his days; but which are now acknowledged almoft every where, except in Spain, Germany, and England. Thefe have ever been the principles of his biographer: but he will not ftoop to examine the ravings of a fublime and

beautiful

4

beautiful apologift for tyranny and fuperftition.

> " A fairer perfon loft not heaven ; he feem'd
> For dignity compos'd, and high exploit :
> But all was falfe and hollow ; though his tongue
> Dropp'd manna, and could make the worfe appear
> The better reafon, to perplex and dafh
> Matureft counfels."

A man formed like Cicero for finging
like a nightingale in a cage, to be kept
for the gratification of luxurious patricians,
now the friend of Pompey, and now of
Cæfar, as it fuited the indulgence of his
inordinate vanity ; fond of words like a
fchool-mafter, and fond of trappings like
a filly little girl let out of a boarding-
fchool. I would indulge him with a copy
of verfes of my own compofition, written
in the ftyle of a madrigal upon my miftrefs's eye-brow.

" Mould'ring

"Mould'ring and frail, to duſt the body tends,
And human greatneſs ſtubborn fortune bends:
Fleeting and vain the ſtoried urns ariſe,
And like a cloud the human vapour flies.
Vain are our buſts and portraits to retain
The ſoul's bright form, and light the lamp again:
By life alone the mimic form revives,
A Tully dead, a Tully yet ſurvives;
Mortal by nature, endleſs in the kind,
Succeſſive ages ſhew the kindred mind."

Fletcher uſed to ſay with Cromwell and Milton, that the trappings of a monarchy and a great ariſtocracy would patch up a very clever little commonwealth. Being in company one day with the witty Dr. Pitcairn, the converſation turned on a perſon of learning whoſe hiſtory was not diſtinctly known. "I knew the man well," ſaid Fletcher: "he was hereditary profeſſor of divinity at Hamburgh." "*Hereditary* profeſſor!" ſaid Pitcairn, with

a laugh

a laugh of aftonifhment and derifion. "Yes, Doctor," replied Fletcher, " heredi- tary profeffor of divinity. What think you of a hereditary king?"

Having faid fo much upon the princi- ples of Fletcher, I think it proper at this juncture of political reform in Europe, that I fhould guard my own expreffed opinions againft popular mifinterpretation on a fubject of fuch great importance to the happinefs of my country.

I have ever thought it was a misfortune to Britain that the Revolution was fol- lowed by fo imperfect a fyftem of political arrangement, and that it would have been more conducive to the future happinefs of the nation, if we had had to erect an entire new fabric of a conftitution in the prefent improved ftate of fociety, than to clear out, patch, and buttrefs the edifice,

as

as has been partially done by the Convention Parliament in the year 1689, by the Bill of Rights, by the Act of Succession, by the Treaty of Union, by the abolition of heritable · jurifdictions and feudal tenures, of perfonal flavery, the confirmation and extenfion of the act of Habeas Corpus, the fecurity of the liberty of fpeech and writing, and of printing, the fecuring private property againft the claims and nullum tempus of the crown, the abridgment of the powers of the ecclefiaftical courts, the abolition of perfonal flavery in Britain, the independency of the falaries of the criminal and civil judges and magiftrates, by the Grenvilian law of elections, the exclufion of tax-gatherers from the right of popular fuffrage in elections of members of parliament, and finally by the declaration of

the

the rights of juries, as judges both of the law and of the fact.

But as things are now fituated, Britain muft be fatisfied to fall at leaft a century behind all other nations, that, like America and France, have had the advantage of erecting a conftitution from the firft foundations of jurifprudence, and of efcaping the dangers that arife from dilapidation.

Had I a crazy old family manfion, I fhould have been better pleafed that my fathers had left me the tafk of erecting a new one, which I might have done cheaper and better than patching the old; but having the manfion, I fhould confider well before I pulled it to the ground. The conftitution of England, Scotland, and Ireland admits of a great and a fafe improvement, which will be foon demanded and obtained by the people, the

equalization

equalization of the rights of election, and the abolition of the rights of primogeniture in private fucceffion. But I would warn my countrymen againft every approach to hafty determination upon the methods of repairing the old houfe, left it fhould tumble about their ears.

When the fanatics, in the year 1567, came to pull down the cathedral of Glafgow, a gardener who ftood by, faid, " My friends, cannot you make it a houfe for ferving your God in your own way? For it would coft your country a great deal to build fuch another." The fanatics defifted, and it is the only cathedral in Scotland, that remains entire and fit for fervice. Such, therefore, with refpect to the Britifh conftitution, is the advice of the gardener of. Dryburgh Abbey. I reject the uniform as I do the principles

G

of

of the Windfor Club, nor will I give any preference to that of Carleton-Houfe, where fenfe and reafon are out of the queftion : but I unaffectedly write in fincerity and truth, what I know to be conducive to the tranquillity and future happinefs of a profperous and induftrious, but corrupted and enervated people.

It was faid of Fletcher, that he wifhed for a republic in which he himfelf fhould rule by his popular talents; but his temper was unaccomodating: nor is there any ground for fuppofing that his views in any tranfaction were felfifh. He was the contriver and mover of the act of the Scotch parliament to ftop any fettlement of the crown until the conftitution was formed, and the rights of the people fecured; and his fpeeches on that occafion will be found in this volume, full of

good

good fenfe, and of manly claffical eloquence.

The Duke of Hamilton was fufpected
of wifhing to embarrafs the fettlement of
the crown, with a view to favour the
eventual pretenfions of his own family.
He went fecretly on board the fhip of
Van Aärfen Somelsdijke, the Dutch admiral in the road of Leith, and propofed an union of Scotland and Holland
as one commonwealth. It may be gueffed
who expected to be vice ftadthölder in
Scotland *. Nothing could be more natural than the averfion the Scots felt to
be funk and loft in the great empire of
Britain; and it was as natural for Hamilton and Fletcher to foment this averfion
with different intentions, and from differ-

* Communicated by Somelsdijke to his relation
Lord Auchenleck, one of the fenators of the College
of Juftice in Scotland.

G 2

ent

ent motives. Lockhart of Carnwath, the memoir writer, flattered himfelf that Fletcher was a Tory, if not a Jacobite, in his heart, becaufe he affociated with Tories and Jacobites: but he did not reflect that the Tories and Jacobites were then the country party, and that Fletcher would hear more from them of the dignity, independence, and intereft of his country, and lefs about a king that infpires a republican with no fentiment but terror or diflike. This, I believe, was the foundation for his being fufpected *of not being a true Whig at bottom*; for Whigs and Tories were in thofe days quite diftinct, difliking and avoiding each other, not mingled together as they now are, to fhare among themfelves the plunder of their country.

From the moft minute examination

of

of the records and memoirs of the times, it fufficiently appears, that while others, whether Whigs or Tories, were endeavouring to turn the Revolution in Britain to the promoting of their own felfifh purpofes, Fletcher neither afked nor obtained' any emolument from the court; but that he was continually attentive to the intereft and honour of Scotland.

When an attempt was made, in the year 1692, to bring about a counter-revolution, Fletcher's ruling principle (though diffatisfied with King William) was the good of his country. He ufed all his influence with the Duke of Hamilton to forget the caufes of his difguft, and to co-operate with the friends of a free conftitution *.

* Vide Fletcher's Letter to the Duke. Dalrymple's Memoirs.

In

In every propofal for the happinefs, and glory of his country, Fletcher was, interefted as if it tended to his own per-fonal emolument and reputation. He was, the firft friend and patron of that extra-ordinary man Paterfon, the projector of the Darien Company; to whofe merits, my kinfman Sir John Dalrymple has done, the juftice they deferve, in the laft volume, of his interefting Memoirs of Great Bri-tain, which, unable as I am to defcribe, with equal fpirit and ability the fhare, Fletcher had in this bufinefs, I fhall give in Sir John's own words.

" Ingenious men draw to each other, like iron and the loadftone : Paterfon, on, his return to London, formed a friend-fhip with Mr. Fletcher of Saltoun, whofe, mind was inflamed with the love of pub-

I   .lic.

lic good, and all of whofe ideas to procure it had a fublimity in them. Fletcher
difliked England merely becaufe he loved
Scotland to excefs; and therefore the report common in Scotland is probably
true, that he was the perfon who perfuaded Paterfon to truft the fate of his
project to his own countrymen alone,
and to let them have the fole benefit,
glory, and danger in it; for in its danger
Fletcher deemed fome of its glory to confift. Although Fletcher had nothing to
hope for, and nothing to fear, becaufe he
had a good eftate, and no children; and
though he was of the country party; yet
in all his fchemes for the public good, he
was in ufe to go as readily to the king's
minifters as to his own friends, being indifferent who had the honour of doing

good,

good, provided it was done. His houfe of Saltoun in Eaft Lothian was near to that of the Marquis of Tweedale, then minifter for Scotland; and they were often together. Fletcher brought Paterfon down to Scotland with him, prefented him to the Marquis, and then, with that power which a vehement fpirit always poffeffes over a diffident one, perfuaded the Marquis, by arguments of public good, and of the honour which would redound to his adminiftration, to adopt the project. Lord Stair and Mr. Johnfton, the two fecretaries of ftate, patronifed thofe abilities in Paterfon which they poffeffed in themfelves; and the lord advocate, Sir James Steuart, the fame man who had adjufted the Prince of Orange's declaration at the Revolution, whofe fon was

married

married to a niece of Lord Stair *, went naturally along with his connections."

FROM this bufy period till the meeting of the Union Parliament, Fletcher

* Anne Dalrymple, daughter of Sir Hugh Dalrymple, lord prefident of the Court of Seffion, was married to Sir James Steuart of Goodtrees, baronet, folicitor general for Scotland, and by him was the mother of the late learned and truly eminent Sir James Steuart Denham, author of the Principles of Political Oeconomy; and four daughters, the fecond of whom, Agnes, of elegant tafte and genius, was the mother of all my father's children, fome of whom inherit her abilities, the ftrong natural parts and probity of the father, with the tafte and brilliant imagination of the mother. " Fortes creantur fortibus & bonis." If this compliment to my brothers fhall appear too ftrong, and be blamed, I look for the reward of Proculeius —" Notus in fratres animi paterni."

was

was uniform and indefatigable in his parliamentary conduct, continually attentive to the rights of the people, and *jealous, as every friend to his country ought to be, of their invasion by the king and his ministers ; for it is as much of the nature of kings and ministers to invade and destroy the rights of the people, as it is of foxes and weasels to rifle a poultry yard, and destroy the poultry.*—All of them therefore ought to be muzzled.

Fletcher was accordingly a strenuous but unsuccefsful advocate for a national militia. His difcourfe on that important fubject written at this time, was not printed until the year 1698. In this Difcourfe he fays, what I wifh I had a voice loud enough to be heard over all Britain and Ireland, to rattle in the ears of the people—" A good and effective militia is of

fuch

fuch importance to a nation, that it is the chief part of the conftitution of any free government. For though, as to other things, the conftitution be ever fo flight, a good militia will always preferve the public liberty. But in the beft conftitution that ever was, as to all other parts of government, if the militia be not upon a right foot, the liberty of that people muft perifh.

" The Swifs," fays he, " at this day are the freeft, happieft, and the people of all Europe who can beft defend themfelves, becaufe they have the beft militia."

What a reproach to the nobility, the gentry, and to the people of Scotland, is it not, that, attending to the dirty confi-deration of pleafing a fub-minifter of Scot-land,

land, they fhould have lately flinched
from forcing the Britifh legiflature to
make them free citizens, and to enjoy
the free ufe of arms in defence of their
own conftitution!

————Pudet hæc opprobria nobis,
Et dici potuiffe, & non potuiffe refelli!

In the year 1703 we find Fletcher
great in the debates concerning the fix-
ing the fucceffion to the crown of Scotland, in the event of Queen Anne's dying
without iffue; which he ftrenuoufly and
fuccefsfully urged the parliament to determine before they fhould think of granting
any fupplies to the crown. It was even
refolved, that the fucceffor to the crown
after Queen Anne, fhould not be the
fame perfon that was King or Queen of
England, *unlefs the juft rights of Scotland*
fhould be declared in parliament at London,

don, and fully settled independent of English interests and councils; and what is remarkable, that wise and excellent, but seemingly very strong rule of the French constitution, that the king or queen should *not* have the power of engaging the nation in war without the consent of parliament, was determined upon by the parliament of Scotland; in the support and preparation of which law, and others for the security of Scottish freedom, Mr. Fletcher had a considerable share, and had great influence by the power of his fervent and manly eloquence. " Prejudice and opinion," said he, " govern the world, to the great distress and ruin of mankind; and though we daily find men so rational as to charm by the disinterested rectitude of their sentiments in all other things, yet, when we touch upon any wrong opinion of theirs

with

with which they have been early prepoffeffed, we find them more irrational
than any thing in nature, and not only
not to be convinced, but obftinately refolved not to hear any reafon againft it.
Thefe prejudices are yet ftronger when
they are taken up by great numbers of
men, who confirm each other through
the courfe of feveral generations, and feem
to have their blood tainted, or, to fpeak
more properly, their animal fpirits influenced by them. Of thefe delufions, one
of the ftrongeft and moft pernicious has
been a violent inclination in many men
to extend the prerogative of the prince to
an abfolute and unlimited power. And
though in limited monarchies all good
men profefs and declare themfelves enemies to all tyrannical practices, yet many
even of thefe are found ready to oppofe

fuch

fuch neceffary limitations as might fecure them from the tyrannical exercife of power in a prince, not only fubject to all the infirmities of other men, but, by the temptations arifing from his power, to far greater. This *humour* * has increafed greatly in the Scottifh nation, fince the union of the crowns in 1603; and the flavifh fubmiffions, which have been made neceffary to procure the favours of the court, have cherifhed and fomented a flavifh principle. I muft put the reprefentatives of the Scots in mind, that no fuch principles were known in this kingdom before the union of the crowns, *and that no monarchy in Europe* was more limited, nor any

* *Humeur*, Scoto-Gallic, fancy, whim. An oppreffed people can never know what the Englifh exhibited of humour *when they were free.*

people

people more jealous of liberty than the Scots *."

Fletcher

* I David Stewart, Earl of Buchan, do throw this gauntlet of Fletcher's down, in the prefence of all England; and if any man fhall take it up, I will try my ftrength with him; but I will not argue with women or priefts, till I fhall fee them leaving their trenches of petticoats and fuperftition, and meeting me on the fair and manly field of hiftorical know-ledge.

Hume told the people of England the truth about their old conftitution, and they called him a Tory. I tell them that Hume was in the right, and I defy them to call *me* a Tory. It was no rarity for the Scots to dethrone a King for attacking the liberties of the people. They difmiffed Baliol becaufe he fold his country; they difmiffed Mary becaufe fhe meant to govern them like the France of the Guifes; they brought in Bruce as the Prince of Orange of Scotland; and for the principles and practice I refer to Buchanan's Dialogue de Jure Regni apud Scotos.

There

Fletcher was by far the moft nervous and correct fpeaker in the parliament of Scotland,

There never was fuch a thing as a peer of Scotland. There were earls indeed, but they did not fit in parliament in right of their earldoms, but in right of their lands; and there they were only on a par with other proprietors of fiefs. James I. of the Scots indeed attempted to introduce the Englifh modes, and was murdered, like Cæfar, by his kinf- man; and James VI. by the ftatute 1587, introduced the practice of the election of reprefentatives for the freeholders; but the nobility, as they were called, *not the peerage* of Scotland, were no more than the barons or freeholders, barons of baron-rent, who by ufage retained their privilege of fitting in parliament in right of their lands, which if they fold, they loft their right of fitting, along with their poffeffions.

There was but one houfe of parliment: and in this, unfortunately for Scotland, the priefts had a privilege to fit in right of their lands. But the Scots had no notion of fuch a monftrous organ of power for their king, as a feparate houfe for his fervants

H

and

Scotland, for he drew his ftyle from the pure models of antiquity, and not from the groffer practical oratory of his contemporaries; fo that his fpeeches and his language will bear a comparifon with the beft fpeeches of the reign of Queen Anne, the Auguftan age of Great Britain, far fuperior to the meretricious, inflated, metaphorical ftyle of our modern orators; from which remark I muft fet down Mr. Charles Fox, member for Weftminfter in the prefent parliament, as a wonderful exception. In many refpects Fox re-

and chaplains, to ftop the progrefs of laws in favour of the rights of the people, before they fhould come to receive the royal affent. As to the idea of a perfect conftitution being to confift of three parts, this was a trinity in which the Scots did not believe; and they fatisfied themfelves with holding the doctrine of the unity, the majefty, and uncontroulable power of the legiflative authority.

— fembles

fembles Fletcher; and may he clofe his career fo as to deferve an equal character!

The irafcibility of Fletcher's temper, and his high fenfe of honour, made him impatient of the flighteft tendency towards an affront. Lord Stair, when fecretary of ftate, having let fall fome expreffions in parliament, that feemed to glance at Fletcher, he feized Stair by the robe, in his place, and gave him the reply valiant. Lord Stair was called to order by the Houfe, and was obliged to afk his pardon publicly.

Fletcher's fpeeches on the confideration of the Treaty of Union being printed in the following fheets of this volume, I fhall only quote a paffage of Alexander Cunningham's hiftory, relating to his appearances on that important occafion. " Andreas Fletferus, ut qui patriam prius

in libertatem vindicaret, bis se in vitæ
discrimen intulerat, nunc vulnus infa-
nabile reipublicæ inferendum, et Scotiam
veluti funere per suos elatam, cernens
hoc tempore extremo, in dicendo effer-
vescit, reginæque ministros vehementer in-
sectatur, et exagitat, nihil res domesticas,
licet amplas, faciens. Sunt qui illius vim
eloquentiæ, etiam in inimicitiis gerendis,
virtutem nimium efferbuisse, & causæ
nocuisse dicunt; *sed quid vetat filium in
funere matris commoveri*, aut civem fortem,
in efferendam funere patriam, dolore gra-
viter inuri, præsertim is qui reipublicæ
commoda suis necessitudinibus semper
potiora duxerat, mortemque pro patria
toties oppetere non dubitaverat? Bu-
chaniæ etiam comes ejusq; patruus Joannes
Areskinus strenue pro patria contende-

bant,

bant, *nihil penſi cum Galliæ factionis ho-
minibus habentes.*"

Fletcher (ſays the anonymous author
of his character in Thomas Rawlinſon's
library) was ſteady in his principles, of
nice honour, great learning; brave as
the ſword he wore; a ſure friend, but an
irreconcileable enemy; and would not
do a baſe thing to eſcape death.

He would not ſubmit to be called either
Whig or Tory, ſaying, *thoſe names were
given and uſed to cloak the knaves of both
parties.* Bravo!

He had acquired the grammatical knowledge of the Italian ſo perfectly 'as to
compoſe and publiſh a treatiſe in that
language; yet he could not ſpeak it, as he
found when having an interview with
Prince Eugene of Savoy, and being ad-

H 3

dreſſed

dreſſed in that language by the Prince, he could not utter a ſyllable to be underſtood. In his perſon he was of low ſtature, thin, of a brown complexion, with piercing eyes; and a gentle frown of keen ſenſibility appeared often upon his countenance.

To the memory of this extraordinary man I have reared this monument. The bodies of men are frail and periſhing: ſo are their portraits and monuments: but, upheld by the power of the Creator, the form of the ſoul is eternal. This cannot be repreſented by ſtatues or by pictures, nor otherwiſe than by a conformity of manners. May whatever was great and truly valuable in Fletcher be for ever imitated by my countrymen, and may the ſplendour of his virtues re-

flect

flect honour upon his family, and glorify
his kindred throughout all generations!

> Ille ego qui quondam patriæ perculfus amore
> Civibus oppreffis libertati fuocurrere aufim,
> Nunc arva paterna colo, fugioq; limina regum.

Dryburgh Abbey,
July 14, 1791.

H 4

APPENDIX.

CONTAINING SOME ACCOUNT OF FLET-
CHER'S FAMILY; AND NOTES EXPLA-
NATORY OF THE LIFE OF FLETCHER.

THE family of Fletcher of Saltoun descends from Sir Bernard Fletcher, a son of Fletcher of Hatton in the county of Cumberland. Robert, his son, established himself in the county of Tweedale. Andrew, the son of Robert, was a merchant at Dundee, in the county of Angus or Forfar. David, the son of Andrew, purchased the estate of Innerpeffer in that county, and married a daughter of Ogilvie of

Pourie,

Pourie, and by her had three sons, Robert, Andrew, and David. Robert died 1613, leaving six sons: Andrew; James, provost of Dundee; Robert, laird of Bencho; Sir George Fletcher of Restenet in Angus-shire; and two others, who died in infancy. Andrew was knighted by James I. 1620; the same year he succeeded his father in the estate of Innerpeffer. He bought the estate of Saltoun in East Lothian, in the year 1643, which had anciently given title to the Lords Abernethy of Saltoun, now represented by the Frasers of Cowie and Philorth, Lords Abernethy of Saltoun. He was one of the senators of the College of Justices in Scotland, by the title of Lord Innerpeffer, as has been mentioned in the life of his grandson; as well as his noble dissent from the surrender of Charles I. to the English army at Newcastle, with Lord

Cardross

Cardrofs and others; who thought the king deferved to be punifhed, but not by thofe to whom he had entrufted the care of his protection.

Lord Innerpeffer was the father of Sir Robert Fletcher of Saltoun, who was the father of the patriot.

———————

With refpect to Fletcher's character in forfaking the Duke of Monmouth at Taunton, the following teftimony of Fergufon, in a MS. quoted by Echard, in his Hiftory of England, ought to be well weighed and confidered before Fletcher be charged with unallowable defertion.

" The Duke of Monmouth was very fenfible of his precipitous adventure into England; but fuffered himfelf to be over-ruled, contrary to both the dictates of his

judgment,

judgment, and the bias of his inclination; for could he have been allowed
to have purfued his own fentiments
and refolutions, he intended to have
fpent that fummer in the court of
Swedeland. But from this he was di-
verted by the importunity of the Earl of
Argyll, and prevailed upon by the advice
and intreaty of the Lord Grey and Mr.
Wade *(contrary to the defires of Mr. Fletcher and Captain Matthews)* to haften
into England. To which I can fay (faith
Mr. Fergufon) I had the leaft acceffion of
any who were about the Duke of Monmouth. Nor would the Earl of Argyll,
after his own *ominous* hafte, fet fail for
Scotland, till he forced a promife from
the Duke of embarking for England within fo many days after. Which the Duke,
rather than fuffer his honour to be ftained,

complied

complied with as far as weather would permit; though he found the obferving his word to interfere with his intereft, as well as all the principles of prudence and difcretion."—My tendernefs for the admirers of King William, and my regard for the illuftrious houfe of Campbell, will not allow me to exprefs what I fufpect in the whole of this tranfaction in Holland. Argyll paid the amende honorable with a vengeance. And the defcendants of Monmouth need not regret the cowardice and perjury of Charles II. nor the failure of poor Monmouth's attempt. It is remarkable that the heir of Monmouth is now the eventual heir general of that very Earl of Argyll, who precipitated the ruin of his patriarch.

SPEECHES

SPEECHES of Mr. FLETCHER

On the QUESTION for the

SETTLEMENT

OF THE

SCOTTISH CROWN,

Delivered in the Scottish Parliament, 1703.

MY LORD CHANCELLOR,

I AM not furprifed to find an act for a fupply brought into this houfe at the beginning of a feffion. I know cuftom has, for a long time, made it common. But, I think, experience might teach us, that fuch acts fhould be the laft of every feffion ; or lie upon the table, till all other great affairs of the nation be finifhed, and then only granted. It is a ftrange pro-

pofition

pofition which is ufually made in this houfe; that if we will give money to the crown, then the crown will give us good laws: as if we were to buy good laws of the crown, and pay money to our princes, that they may do their duty, and comply with their coronation oath. And yet this is not the worft; for we have often had promifes of good laws, and when we have given the fums demanded, thofe promifes have been broken, and the nation left to feek a remedy; which is not to be found, unlefs we obtain the laws we want, before we give a fupply. And if this be a fufficient reafon at all times to poftpone a money-act, can we be blamed for doing fo at this time, when the duty we owe to our country indifpenfably obliges us to provide for the common fafety in cafe of an event, altogether out

of

of our power, and which muſt neceſſarily diſſolve the government, unleſs we continue and ſecure it by new laws ; I mean the death of her majeſty, which God in his mercy long avert? I move, therefore, that the houſe would take into conſideration what acts are neceſſary to ſecure our religion, liberty, and trade, in caſe of the ſaid event, before any act of ſupply, or other buſineſs whatever be brought into deliberation.

Act concerning offices, &c. brought in by the ſame member.

'THE eſtates of parliament taking 'into their conſideration, that, to the 'great loſs and detriment of this nation, 'great ſums of money are yearly carried

I   'out

' out of it, by thofe who wait and depend
' at court, for places and preferments in
' this kingdom : and that by Scotfmen,
' employing Englifh intereft at court, in
' order to obtain their feveral pretenfions,
' this nation is in hazard of being brought
' to depend upon Englifh minifters : and
' likewife confidering, that by reafon our
' princes do no more refide amongft us,
' they cannot be rightly informed of the
' merit of perfons pretending to places,
' offices, and penfions; therefore our fo-
' vereign lady, with advice and confent
' of the eftates of parliament, ftatutes and
' ordains, that after the deceafe of her
' majefty, whom God long preferve, and
' heirs of her body failing, all places and
' offices both civil and military, and all
' penfions, formerly conferred by our
kings,

' kings, shall ever after be given by par-
' liament, by way of ballot.'

II.

MY LORD CHANCELLOR,

WHEN our kings succeeded to the crown of England, the ministers of that nation took a short way to ruin us, by concurring with their inclinations to extend the prerogative in Scotland; and the great places and pensions conferred upon Scotsmen by that court, made them to be willing instruments in the work. From that time this nation began to give away their privileges one after the other, though they then stood more in need of having them enlarged. And as the col-

 lections

lections of our laws, before the Union of the Crowns, are full of acts to secure our liberty, thofe laws that have been made since that time are directed chiefly to extend the prerogative. And that we might not know what rights and liberties were ftill ours, nor be excited by the memory of what our anceftors enjoyed, to recover thofe we had loft, in the two laft editions of our acts of parliament the moft confiderable laws for the liberty of the fubject are induftriously and defignedly left out. All our affairs fince the Union of the Crowns have been managed by the advice of Englifh minifters, and the principal offices of the kingdom filled with fuch men as the court of England knew would be fubfervient to their defigns: by which means they have had fo vifible an influence upon our whole adminiftration,

that

that we have, from that time, appeared to the reſt of the world more like a conquered province, than a free independent people. The account is very ſhort: whilſt our princes are not abſolute in England, they muſt be influenced by that nation, our miniſters muſt follow the directions of the prince, or loſe their places, and our places and penſions will be diſtributed according to the inclinations of a king of England, ſo long as a king of England has the diſpoſal of them: neither ſhall any man obtain the leaſt advancement, who refuſes to vote in council and parliament under that influence. So that there is no way to free this country from a ruinous dependance upon the Engliſh court, unleſs by placing the power of conferring offices and penſions in the parliament, ſo long as we ſhall have the

I 3 ſame

same-king with England. The ancient kings of Scotland, and even those of France, had not the power of conferring the chief offices of state, though each of them had only one kingdom to govern, and that the difficulty we labour under, of two kingdoms which have different interests governed by the same king, did not occur. Besides, we all know that the disposal of our places and pensions is so considerable a thing to a king of England, that several of our princes, since the Union of the Crowns, have wished to be free from the trouble of deciding between the many pretenders. That which would have given them ease, will give us liberty, and make us significant to the common interest of both nations. Without this, it is impossible to free us from a dependence on the English court: all other re-

medies

medies and conditions of government will prove ineffectual, as plainly appears from the nature of the thing; for who is not sensible of the influence of places and pensions upon all men and all affairs? If our ministers continue to be appointed by the English court, and this nation may not be permitted to dispose of the offices and places of this kingdom to balance the English bribery, they will corrupt every thing to that degree, that if any of our laws stand in their way they will get them repealed. Let no man say, that it cannot be proved, that the English court has ever bestowed any bribe in this country. For they bestow all offices and pensions; they bribe us, and are masters of us at our own cost. It is nothing but an English interest in this house, that those, who wish well to

I 4

our

our country have to ſtruggle with at this
time. We may, if we pleaſe, dream of other
remedies; but ſo long as Scotſmen muſt
go to the Engliſh court to obtain offices
of truſt or profit in this kingdom, thoſe
offices will always be managed with regard to the court and intereſt of England,
though to the betraying of the intereſt of
this nation, whenever it comes in com-
petition with that of England. And
what leſs can be expected, unleſs we re-
ſolve to expect miracles, and that greedy,
ambitious, and for the moſt part neceſſi-
tous men, involved in great debts, bur-
dened with great families, and having
great titles to ſupport, will lay down their
places, rather than comply with an Engliſh
intereſt in obedience to the prince's commands? Now, to find Scotſmen oppoſing
this, and willing that Engliſh miniſters,

for

for this is the cafe, fhould have the difpofal of places and penfions in Scotland, rather than their own parliament, is matter of great aftonifhment; but that it fhould be fo much as a queftion in the parliament, is altogether incomprehenfible: and if an indifferent perfon were to judge, he would certainly fay we were an Englifh parliament. Every man knows that princes give places and penfions by the influence of thofe who advife them. So that the queftion comes to no more than, whether this nation would be in a better condition, if, in conferring our places and penfions, the prince fhould be determined by the parliament of Scotland, or by the minifters of a court, that make it their intereft to keep us low and miferable. We all know that this is the caufe of our poverty, mifery and dependence. But we have been

for

for a long time fo poor, fo miferable, and
depending, that we have neither heart nor
courage, though we want not the means,
to free ourfelves.

III.

MY LORD CHANCELLOR,

PREJUDICE and opinion govern the
world, to the great diftrefs and ruin of
mankind; and though we daily find men
fo rational as to charm by the difinterefted
rectitude of their fentiments in all other
things, yet when we touch upon any
wrong opinion with which they have
been early prepoffeffed, we find them
more irrational than any thing in nature;
and not only not to be convinced, but
obftinately refolved not to hear any reafon
againft it. Thefe prejudices are yet ftronger

when

when they are taken up by great numbers of men, who confirm each other
through the courfe of feveral generations,
and feem to have their blood tainted, or,
to fpeak more properly, their animal fpirits
influenced by them. Of thefe delufions,
one of the ftrongeft, and moft pernicious,
has been a violent inclination in many
men to extend the prerogative of the
prince to an abfolute and unlimited power.
And though, in limited monarchies, all
good men profefs and declare themfelves
enemies to all tyrannical practices, yet
many, even of thefe, are found ready to
oppofe fuch neceffary limitations as might
fecure them from the tyrannical exercife
of power in a prince, not only fubject to
all the infirmities of other men, but, by
the temptations arifing from his power,
to far greater. This humour has greatly

increafed

increased in our nation, since the Union of the Crowns; and the slavish submissions, which have been made necessary to procure the favours of the court, have cherished and fomented a slavish principle. But I must take leave to put the representatives of this nation in mind, that no such principles were in this kingdom before the Union of the Crowns; and that no monarchy in Europe was more limited, nor any people more jealous of liberty than the Scots. These principles were first introduced among us after the Union of the Crowns, and the prerogative extended to the overthrow of our ancient constitution, chiefly by the prelatical party; though the peevish, imprudent, and detestable conduct of the presbyterians, who opposed these principles only in others, drove many into them, gave them greater

force,

force, and rooted them more deeply in this nation. Should we not be afhamed to embrace opinions contrary to reafon, and contrary to the fentiments of our anceftors, merely upon account of the uncharitable and infupportable humour and ridiculous conduct of bigots of any fort? If then no fuch principles were in this nation, and the conftitution of our government had greatly limited the prince's power before the Union of the Crowns; dare any man fay he is a Scotfman, and refufe his confent to reduce the government of this nation, after the expiration of the intail, within the fame limits as before that union? And if, fince the Union of the Crowns, every one fees that we ftand in need of more limitations; will any man act in fo direct an oppofition to his own reafon, and the un-

doubted

doubted intereſt of his country, as not
to concur in limiting the government yet
more than before the Union, particularly
by the addition of this ſo neceſſary limitation for which I am now ſpeaking?
My Lord, theſe are ſuch clear demon-
ſtrations of what we ought to do in ſuch
conjunctures, that all men of common ingenuity muſt be aſhamed of entering into
any other meaſures. Let us not then
tread in the ſteps of mean and fawning
prieſts of any ſort, who are always dif-
poſed to place an abſolute power in the
prince, if he on his part will gratify their
ambition, and by all means ſupport their
form of church-government, to the perſe-
cution of all other men, who will not
comply with their impoſitions. Let us
begin where our anceſtors left off before
the Union of the Crowns, and be for the
future,

future, more jealous of our liberties, becaufe there is more need. But I muft
take upon me to fay, that he who is not
for fetting great limitations upon the
power of the prince, particularly that for
which I am fpeaking, in cafe we have the
fame king with England, can act by no
principle, whether he be a prefbyterian,
prelatical, or prerogative man, for the
court of St. Germains, or that of Hanover; I fay, he can act by no principle
unlefs that of being a flave to the court
of England for his own advantage. And
therefore let not thofe, who go under
the name of prerogative-men, cover themfelves with the pretext of principles in
this cafe; for fuch men are plainly for
the prerogative of the Englifh court over
this nation, becaufe this limitation is de-

manded

manded-;only in cafe we come to have
the fame king with England.

———————

*Act for the fecurity of the kingdom, brought
in by the fame member.*

'THE eftates of parliament confider-
'ing, that when it fhall pleafe God to
'afflict this nation with the death of our
'fovereign lady the queen (whom God of
'his infinite mercy long preferve) if the
'fame fhall happen to be without heirs
'of her body, this kingdom may fall into
'great confufion and diforder before a fuc-
'ceffor can be declared. For preventing
'thereof, our fovereign lady, with advice
'and confent of the eftates of parliament,
'ftatutes and ordains, that if, at the afore-
'faid time, any parliament or convention

of

‘ of eftates fhall be affembled, then the
‘ members of that parliament or conven-
‘ tion of eftates fhall take the adminiftra-
‘ tion of the government upon them:
‘ excepting thofe barons and boroughs,
‘ who, at the aforefaid time, fhall have
‘ any place or penfion, mediately or im-
‘ mediately, of the crown: whofe com-
‘ miffions are hereby declared to be void;
‘ and that new members fhall be chofen
‘ in their place: but if there be no parlia-
‘ ment or convention of eftates actually
‘ affembled, then the members of the cur-
‘ rent parliament fhall affemble with all
‘ poffible diligence: and if there be no
‘ current parliament, then the members
‘ of the laft diffolved parliament, or con-
‘ vention of eftates, fhall affemble in like
‘ manner: and in thofe two laft cafes, fo
‘ foon as there fhall be one hundred

K   ‘ members

' members met, in which number the ba-
' rons and boroughs before-mentioned are
' not to be reckoned, they fhall take the
' adminiftration of the government upon
' them: but neither they, nor the mem-
' bers of parliament or convention of
' eftates, if at the time aforefaid affem-
' bled, fhall proceed to the weighty affair
' of naming and declaring a fucceffor, till
' twenty days after they have affumed
' the adminiftration of the government:
' both that there may be time for all the
' other members to come to Edinburgh,
' which is hereby declared the place of
' their meeting, and for the election of
' new barons and boroughs in place above-
' mentioned. But fo foon as the twenty
' days are elapfed, then they fhall proceed
' to the publifhing, by proclamation, the
' conditions of government, on which
                              ' they

' they will receive the fucceffor 'to the
' imperial crown of this realm; which,
' in the cafe only of our being under the.
' fame king with England, are as follow.

1. ' That elections fhall be ·made at'
' every Michaelmas head-court for a new
' parliament every year: to fit the firft of
' November next following, and adjourn
' themfelves from time to time, till next
' Michaelmas: that they choofe their own
' prefident, and that every thing fhall be
' determined by balloting, in place of
' voting.

2. ' That fo many leffer barons fhall
' be added to the parliament, as there
' have been noblemen created fince the
' laft augmentation of the number of the
' barons; and that in all time coming, for
' every nobleman that fhall be created,

K 2 ' there

' there shall be a baron added to the par-
' liament.

3. ' That no man have vote in par-
' liament but a nobleman or elected
' member.

4. ' That the king shall give the fanc-
' tion to all laws offered by the estates;
' and that the president of the parliament
' be impowered by his majesty to give
' the fanction in his absence, and have
' ten pounds sterling a day salary.

5. ' That a committee of one and
' thirty members, of which nine to be a
' quorum, chosen out of their own num-
' ber, by every parliament, shall, during
' the intervals of parliament, under the
' king, have the administration of the
' government, be his council, and ac-
' countable to the next parliament; with
power

' power on extraordinary occasions to
' call the parliament together: and that
' in the said council, all things be deter-
' mined by balloting in place of voting.

6. ' That the king, without consent
' of parliament, shall not have the power
' of making peace and war; or that of
' concluding any treaty with any other
' state or potentate.

7. ' That all places and offices, both
' civil and military, and all pensions for-
' merly conferred by our kings, shall ever
' after be given by parliament.

8. ' That no regiment or company of
' horse, foot, or dragoons, be kept on foot
' in peace or war, but by consent of par-
' liament.

9. ' That all the fencible men of the
' nation, betwixt sixty and sixteen, be,
' with all diligence possible, armed with

K 3 ' bayonets,

‘ bayonets, and firelocks all of a caliber,
‘ and continue always provided in such
‘ arms, with ammunition suitable.

10. ‘ That no general indemnity, nor
‘ pardon for any tranfgreffion againft the
‘ public, fhall be valid without confent
‘ of parliament.

11. ‘ That the fifteen fenators of the
‘ College of Juftice fhall be incapable of
‘ being members of parliament, or of any
‘ other office, or any penfion: but the
‘ falary that belongs to their place to be
‘ increafed as the parliament fhall think
‘ fit: that the office of prefident fhall be
‘ in three of their number to be named
‘ by parliament, and that there be no
‘ extraordinary lords. And alfo, that the
‘ lords of the juftice-court fhall be diftinct
‘ from thofe of the feffion, and under the
‘ fame reftrictions.

12. ‘ That

12. 'That if any king break in upon any
' of these conditions of government, he
' shall, by the estates, be declared to have
' forfeited the crown.

' Which proclamation made, they are
' to go on to the naming and declaring
' a successor: and when he is declared,
' if present, are to read to him the claim
' of right and conditions of government
' above-mentioned, and to desire of him,
' that he may accept the crown accord-
' ingly; and he accepting, they are to
' administer to him the oath of corona-
' tion: but if the successor be not present,
' they are to delegate such of their own
' number as they shall think fit, to see
' the same performed, as said is: and
' are to continue in the administration
' of the government, until the successor's
' accepting of the crown, upon the afore-

K 4 ' said

' faid terms, be known to them : where-
' upon having then a king at their head,
' they fhall, by his authority, declare them-
' felves a parliament, and proceed to the
' doing of whatever fhall be thought ex-
' pedient for the welfare of the realm. And
' it is likewife, by the authority aforefaid,
' declared, that if her prefent majefty
' fhall think fit, during her own time,
' with the advice and confent of the
' eftates of parliament, failing heirs of her
' body, to declare a fucceffor, yet never-
' thelefs, after her majefty's deceafe, the
' members of parliament or convention
' fhall, in the feveral cafes, and after the
' manner above fpecified, meet and admit
' the fucceffor to the government, in the
' terms, and after the manner, as faid is.
' And it is hereby further declared, that
' after the deceafe of her majefty, and

' failing

'failing heirs of her body, the foremen-
'tioned manner and method ſhall, in the
'ſeveral caſes, be that of declaring and
'admitting to the government all thoſe
'who ſhall hereafter ſucceed to the im-
'perial crown of this realm ; and that it
'ſhall be high treaſon for any man to
'own or acknowledge any perſon as king
'or queen of this realm, till they are
'declared and admitted in the above-
'mentioned manner, And laſtly, it is
'hereby declared, that by the death of
'her majeſty, or any of her ſucceſſors,
'all commiſſions, both civil and military,
'fall and are void; and that this act
'ſhall come in place of the ſeventeenth
'act of the ſixth ſeſſion of king William's
'parliament. And all acts and laws, that
'any way derogate from this preſent act,

'' are

' are hereby in fo far declared void and
' abrogated.'

IV.

My Lord Chancellor,

IT is the utmoft height of human prudence to fee and embrace every favourable
opportunity: and if a word fpoken in
feafon does, for the moft part, produce
wonderful effects; of what confequence
and advantage muft it be to a nation in
deliberations of the higheft moment; in
occafions, when paft, for ever irretrievable,
to enter into the right path, and take
hold of the golden opportunity which
makes the moft arduous things eafy, and
without which the moft inconfiderable
may put a ftop to all our affairs? We

7　　　　　　　　　　　have

have this day an opportunity in our hands
which if we manage to the advantage
of the nation we have the honour to reprefent, we may, fo far as the viciffitude
and uncertainty of human affairs will
permit, be for many ages eafy and happy.
But if we defpife or neglect this occafion,
we have voted our perpetual dependence
on another nation.   If men could always
retain thofe juft impreffions of things
they at fome times have upon their minds,
they would be much more fteady in their
actions.   And as I may boldly fay, that
no man is to be found in this houfe,
who, at fome time or other, has not had
that juft fenfe of the miferable condition
to which this nation is reduced by a dependence upon the Englifh court, I fhould
demand no more but the like impreffions
at this time to pafs all the limitations
mentioned

mentioned in the draught of an act I have already brought into this houfe; fince they are not limitations upon any prince, who fhall only be king of Scotland, nor do any way tend to feparate us from England; but calculated merely to this end, that fo long as we continue to be under the fame prince with our neigh-bour nation, we may be free from the influence of Englifh councils and mini-fters; that the nation may not be im-poverifhed by an expenfive attendance at court, and that the force and exercife of our government may be, as far as is poffible, within ourfelves. By which means trade, manufactures, and hufbandry will flourifh, and the affairs of the nation be no longer neglected, as they have been hitherto.

Thefe are the ends to which all the limi-tations

tations are directed, that English councils may not hinder the acts of our parliaments from receiving the royal assent; that we may not be engaged without our consent in the quarrels they may have with other nations; that they may not obstruct the meeting of our parliaments, nor interrupt their sitting; that we may not stand in need of posting to London for places and pensions, by which, whatever particular men may get, the nation must always be a loser; nor apply for the remedies of our grievances to a court, where, for the most part, none are to be had. On the contrary, if these conditions of government be enacted, our constitution will be amended, and our grievances be easily redressed by a due execution of our own laws, which to this day we have never been able to obtain. The best and

wisest

wifeſt men in England will be glad to
hear that theſe limitations are ſettled by
us. For though the ambition of courtiers
lead them to deſire an uncontroulable
power at any rate; yet wiſer men will
conſider, that when two nations live under the ſame prince, the condition of the
one cannot be made intolerable, but a ſe-
paration muſt inevitably follow, which
will be dangerous if not deſtructive to
both. The ſenate of Rome wiſely determined in the buſineſs of the Privernates,
that all people would take hold of the firſt
opportunity to free themſelves from an
uneaſy condition; that no peace could be
laſting, in which both parties did not find
their account; and that no alliance was
ſtrong enough to keep two nations in
amity, if the condition of either were
made worſe by it. For my own part,

my

my lord chancellor, before i will confent to continue in our prefent miferable and languifhing condition after the deceafe of her majefty, and heirs of her body failing, I fhall rather give my vote for a fe-paration from England at any rate. I hope no man, who is now poffeffed of an office, will take umbrage at thefe conditions of government, though fome of them feem to diminifh, and others do entirely fupprefs the place he poffeffes : for befides the fcandal of preferring a private intereft before that of our country, thefe limitations are not to take place immediately. The queen is yet young, and by the grace of God may live many years, I hope longer than all thofe fhe has placed in any truft; and fhould we not be happy, if thofe who, for the future, may defign to recommend themfelves for any office,

could

could not do it by any other way than the favour of this houfe, which they who appear for thefe conditions well deferve in a more eminent degree? Would we rather court an Englifh minifter for a place than a parliament of Scotland? Are we afraid of being taken out of the hands of Englifh courtiers, and left to govern ourfelves? And do we doubt whether an Englifh miniftry or a Scots parliament will be moft for the intereft of Scotland? But that which feems moft difficult in this queftion, and in which if fatisfaction be given, I hope no man will pretend to be diffatisfied with thefe limitations, is the intereft of a king of Great Britain. And here I fhall take liberty to fay, that as the limitations do no way affect any prince that may be king of Scotland only, fo they will be found highly advantageous

.to

to a king of Great Britain. Some of our
late kings, when they have been per-
plexed about the affairs of Scotland, did
let fall such expreſſions as intimated they
thought them not worth their application.
And indeed we ought not to wonder if
princes, like other men, ſhould grow
weary of toiling where they find no advantage. But to ſet this affair in a true
light: I deſire to know, whether it can be
more advantageous to a king of Great
Britain to have an unlimited prerogative
over this country, in our preſent ill condition, which turns to no account, than
that this nation, grown rich and powerful
under theſe conditions of government,
ſhould be able upon any emergency to
furniſh a good body of land forces, with
a ſquadron of ſhips for war, all paid by
ourſelves, to aſſiſt his majeſty in the wars

L   he

he may undertake for the defence of the
proteftant religion and liberties of Europe.
Now, fince I hope I have fhewn, that
thofe who are for the prerogative of the
kings of Scotland, and all thofe who are
poffeffed of places at this time, together
with the whole Englifh nation, as well as
a king of Great Britain, have caufe to be
fatisfied with thefe regulations of government, I would know what difficulty can
remain; unlefs that, being accuftomed to
live in a dependency, and unacquainted
with liberty, we know not fo much as the
meaning of the word; nor, if that fhould
be explained to us, can ever perfuade ourfelves we fhall obtain the thing, though
we have it in our power, by a few votes,
to fet ourfelves and our pofterity free. To
fay that this will ftop at the royal affent,
is a fuggeftion difrefpectful to her majefty,

and

and which ought neither to be mentioned in parliament, nor be confidered by any member of this houfe. And, were this a proper time, I am confident I could fay fuch things as, being reprefented to the queen, would convince her, that no perfon can have greater intereft, nor obtain more lafting honour, by the enacting of thefe conditions of government, than her majefty. And if the nation be affifted in this exigency by the good offices of his grace the high commiffioner, I fhall not doubt to affirm, that in procuring this bleffing to our country from her majefty, he will do more for us, than all the great men of that noble family, of which he is defcended, ever did; though it feems to have been their peculiar province for divers ages, to defend the liberties of this nation againft the power of the Englifh

L 2

and

and the deceit of courtiers. What further arguments can I ufe to perfuade this houfe to enact thefe limitations, and embrace this occafion, which we have fo little de- ferved? I might bring many; but the moft proper and effectual to perfuade all, I take to be this: that our anceftors did enjoy the moft effential liberties contained in the act I propofed: and though fome few of lefs moment are among them which they had not, yet they were in poffeffion of divers others not contained in thefe articles: that they enjoyed thefe privileges when they were feparated from England, had their prince living among them, and confequently ftood not in fo great need of thefe limitations. Now, fince we have been under the fame prince with England, and therefore ftand in the greateft need of them, we have not only

neglected

neglected to make a due provision of that kind, but in divers parliaments have given away our liberties, and upon the matter subjected this crown to the court of England; and are become so accustomed to depend on them, that we seem to doubt whether we shall lay hold of this happy opportunity to resume our freedom. If nothing else will move us, at least let us not act in opposition to the light of our own reason and conscience, which daily represents to us the ill constitution of our government, the low condition into which we are sunk, and the extreme poverty, distress, and misery of our people. Let us consider whether we will have the nation continue in these deplorable circumstances, and lose this opportunity of bringing freedom and plenty among us. Sure the heart of every honest man must bleed daily, to

L 3

see

fee the mifery in which our commons,
and even many of our gentry, live; which
has no other caufe but the ill conftitution,
of our government, and our bad government no other root but our dependence
upon the court of England.   If our kings
lived among us, it would not be ftrange
to find thefe limitations rejected.   It is
not the prerogative of a king of Scotland
I would diminifh, but the prerogative of
Englifh minifters over this nation.   To
conclude, thefe conditions of government
being either fuch as our anceftors enjoyed,
or principally directed to cut off our dependence on an Englifh court, and not to
take place during the life of the queen;
he who refufes his confent to them, whatever he may be by birth, cannot fure be a
Scotfman by affection. This will be a true
teft to diftinguifh, not whig from tory,

7   prefby-

prefbyterian from epifcopal, Hanover from St. Germains, nor yet a courtier from a man out of place; but a proper teft to diftinguifh a friend from an enemy to his country. And indeed we are fplit into fo many parties, and cover ourfelves with fo many falfe pretexts, that fuch a teft feems neceffary to bring us into the light, and fhew every man in his own colours. In a word, my lord chancellor, we are to confider, that though we fuffer under many grievances, yet our dependence upon the court of England is the caufe of all, comprehends them all, and is the band that ties up the bundle. If we break this, they will all drop and fall to the ground: if not, this band will ftraiten us more and more, till we fhall be no longer a people.

I therefore humbly propofe, that, for the fecurity of our religion, liberty, and

L 4

trade,

trade, thefe limitations be declared, by a refolution of this houfe, to be the conditions, upon which the nation will receive a fucceffor to the crown of this realm, after the deceafe of her prefent majefty, and failing heirs of her body, in cafe the faid fucceffor fhall be alfo king or queen of England.

V.

My Lord Chancellor,

I AM forry to hear what has been juft now fpoken from the throne. I know the duty I owe to her majefty, and the refpect that is due to her commiffioner; and therefore fhall fpeak with a juft regard to both. But the duty I owe to my country obliges me to fay, that what we have now heard from the throne, muft of neceffity

proceed

proceed from Englifh councils. If we had demanded, that thefe limitations fhould take place during the life of her majefty, or of the heirs of her body, perhaps we might have no great reafon to complain, though they fhould be refufed. But that her majefty fhould prefer the prerogative of fhe knows not who, to the happinefs of the whole people of Scotland; that fhe fhould deny her affent to fuch conditions of government as are not limitations upon the crown of Scotland, but only fuch as are abfolutely neceffary to relieve us from a fubjection to the court of England, muft proceed from Englifh councils; as well becaufe there is no Scots minifter now at London, as becaufe I have had an account, which I believe to be too well grounded, that a letter to this effect has been fent down hither by the lord treafurer

furer of England, not many days ago.
Befides, all men who have lately been at
London well know, that nothing has been
more common, than to fee Scotfmen of
the feveral parties addreffing themfelves
to Englifh minifters about Scots affairs;
and even to fome ladies of that court,
whom, for the refpect I bear to their relations, I fhall not name. Now, whether
we fhall continue under the influence and
fubjection of the Englifh court; or whether it be not high time to lay before her
majefty, by a vote of this houfe, the conditions of government upon which we
will receive a fucceffor, I leave to the
wifdom of the parliament. This I muft
fay, that to tell us any thing of her majefty's intentions in this affair, before we
have prefented any act to that purpofe for
the royal affent, is to prejudge the caufe,

and

and altogether unparliamentary. I will add, that nothing has ever shewn the power and force of Englifh councils upon our affairs in a more eminent manner at any time, fince the union of the crowns. No man in this houfe is more convinced of the great advantage of that peace which both nations enjoy by living under one prince. But as, on the one hand, fome men, for private ends, and in order to get into offices, have either neglected or betrayed the intereft of this nation, by a mean compliance with the Englifh court; fo on the other fide it cannot be denied, that we have been but indifferently ufed by the Englifh nation. I fhall not infift upon the affair of Darien, in which, by their means and influence chiefly, we fuffered fo great a lofs both in men and money, as to put us almoft beyond hope

of

of ever having any confiderable trade; and this contrary to their own true intereft, which now appears but too vifibly. I fhall not go about to enumerate inftances of a provoking nature in other matters, but keep myfelf precifely to the thing we are upon. The Englifh nation did, fome time paft, take into confideration the nomination of a fucceffor to that crown; an affair of the higheft importance, and, one would think, of common concernment to both kingdoms. Did they ever require our concurrence? Did they ever defire the late king to caufe the parliament of Scotland to meet, in order to take our advice and confent? Was not this to tell us plainly, that we ought to be concluded by their determinations, and were not worthy to be confulted in the matter? Indeed, my lord chancellor, confidering

their

their whole carriage in this affair, and the broad infinuations we have now heard, that we are not to expect her majefty's affent to any limitations on a fucceffor (which muft proceed from Englifh councils), and confidering we cannot propofe to ourfelves any other relief from that fervitude we lie under by the influence of that court; it is my opinion, that the houfe come to a refolution, *That after the deceafe of her majefty, heirs of her body failing, we will feparate our crown from that of England.*

VI.

MY LORD CHANCELLOR,

THAT there fhould be limitations on a fucceffor, in order to take away our dependence on the court of England, if both

nations

nations fhould have the fame king, no
man here feems to oppofe.   And I think
very few will be of opinion, that fuch
limitations fhould be deferred till the meeting of the nation's reprefentatives upon
the deceafe of her majefty.   For if the
fucceffor be not named before that' time,
every one will be fo earneft to promote
the pretenfions of the perfon he moft
affects, that new conditions will be altogether forgotten.   So that thofe who are
only in appearance for thefe limitations,
and in reality againft them, endeavour for
their laft refuge to miflead well-meaning
men, by telling them, that it is not ad-
vifable to put them into the act of fecurity,
as well for fear of lofing all, as becaufe
they will be more conveniently placed in
a feparate act.   My lord chancellor, I
would fain know if any thing can be
                                              more

more proper in an act which appoints the naming and manner of admitting a fuc- ceffor, than the conditions on which we agree to receive him. I would know, if the deferring of any thing, at a time when naturally it fhould take place, be not to put a flur upon it, and an endeavour to defeat it. And if the limitations in quef- tion are pretended to be fuch a burden in the act, as to hazard the lofs of the whole, can we expect to obtain them when fe- parated from the act? Is there any com- mon fenfe in this? Let us not deceive our- felves, and imagine that the act of 1696 does not expire immediately after the queen and heirs of her body; for in all that act, the heirs and fucceffors of his late majefty king William are always reftrained and fpecified by thefe exprefs words, ' ac- ' cording to the declaration of the eftates,

' dated

‘ dated the 11th of April 1689.’ So that, unlefs we make a due provifion by fome new law, a diffolution of the government will enfue immediately upon the death of her majefty, failing heirs of her body. Such an act therefore being of abfolute and indifpenfable neceffity, I am of opinion, that the limitations ought to be inferted therein as the only proper place for them, and fureft way to obtain them: and that whoever would feparate them, does not fo much defire we fhould obtain the act, as that we fhould lofe the limitations.

VII.

MY LORD CHANCELLOR,

I HOPE I need not inform this honourable houfe, that all acts which can be proposed

pofed

pofed for the security of this kingdom,
are vain and empty propofitions, unlefs
they are fupported by arms; and that to
rely upon any law, without fuch a fecurity, is to lean upon a fhadow. We had
better never pafs this act: for then we fhall
not imagine we have done any thing for
our fecurity; and if we think we can do
any thing effectual without that provifion,
we deceive ourfelves, and are in a moft
dangerous condition. Such an act cannot
be faid to be an act for the fecurity of
any thing, in which the moft neceffary
claufe is wanting, and without which all
the reft is of no force: neither can any
'kingdom be really fecured but by arming
the people.   Let no man pretend that we
have ftanding forces to fupport this law;
and that, if their numbers be not fufficient,
we may raife more. It is very well known .

M

this

this nation cannot maintain so many standing forces as would be necessary for our
defence, though we could entirely rely
upon their fidelity. The possession of arms
is the distinction of a freeman from a
slave. He who has nothing, and belongs
to another, must be defended by him, and
needs no arms: but he who thinks he is
his own master, and has any thing he
may call his own, ought to have arms to
defend himself and what he possesses, or
else he lives precariously and at discretion.
And though for a while those who have
the sword in their power abstain from
doing him injuries; yet, by degrees, he
will be awed into a submission to every arbitrary command. Our ancestors, by being
always armed, and frequently in action,
defended themselves against the Romans,
Danes, and English ; and maintained their
liberty

liberty againſt the incroachments of their own princes. If we are not rich enough to pay a ſufficient number of ſtanding forces, we have at leaſt this advantage, that arms in our own hands ſerve no leſs to maintain our liberty at home, than to defend us from enemies abroad. Other nations, if they think they can truſt ſtanding forces, may, by their means, defend themſelves againſt foreign enemies. But we, who have not wealth ſufficient to pay ſuch forces, ſhould not, of all nations under heaven, be unarmed. For us then to continue without arms, is to be directly in the condition of ſlaves: to be found unarmed, in the event of her majeſty's death, would be to have no manner of ſecurity for our liberty, property, or the independence of this kingdom. By being unarmed, we every day run the riſk of our

M 2

all,

all, fince we know not how foon that event may overtake us: to continue ftill unarmed, when, by this very act now under deliberation, we have put a cafe, which happening may feparate us from England, would be the groffeft of all follies. And if we do not provide for arming the kingdom in fuch an exigency, we fhall become a jeft and a proverb to the world.

———————

VIII.

My Lord Chancellor,

IF in the fad event of her majefty's deceafe without heirs of her body, any confiderable military force fhould be in the hands of one or more men, who might have an underftanding together, we are not very fure what ufe they would make

of

of them in fo nice and critical a conjunc-
ture. We know, that as the moft juft and
honourable enterprifes, when they fail,
are accounted in the number of rebellions;
fo all attempts, however unjuft, if they
fucceed, always purge themfelves of all
guilt and imputation. If a man prefume
he fhall have fuccefs, and obtain the utmoft
of his hopes, he will not too nicely examine the point of right, nor balance too
fcrupuloufly the injury he does to his
country. I would not have any man take
this for a reflection upon thofe honourable perfons, who have at prefent the
command of our troops. For, befides
that we are not certain who fhall be in
thofe commands at the time of fuch an
event, we are to know that all men are
frail, and the wicked and mean-fpirited
world has paid too much honour to many,

M 3

who

who have fubverted the liberties of their
country. We fee a great difpofition at this
time in fome men, not to confent to any
limitations on a fucceffor, though we
fhould name the fame with England.
And therefore fince this is probably the
laft opportunity we fhall ever have of
freeing ourfelves from our dependence on
the Englifh court, we ought to manage it
with the utmoft jealoufy and diffidence
of fuch men. For though we have ordered the nation to be armed and exer-
cifed, which will be a fufficient defence
when done; yet we know not but the
event, which God avert, may happen before this can be effected. And we may
eafily imagine, what a few bold men, at
the head of a fmall number of regular
troops, might do, when all things are in
confufion and fufpenfe. So that we ought

L   to

to make effectual provision, with the utmoft circumfpection, that all fuch forces may be fubfervient to the government and intereft of this nation, and not to the private ambition of their commanders. I therefore move, that immediately upon the deceafe of her majefty, all military commiffions above that of a captain be null and void.

IX.

My Lord Chancellor,

I KNOW it is the undoubted prerogative of her majefty, that no act of this houfe fhall have the force of a law without her royal affent. And as I am confident his grace the high commiffioner is fufficiently inftructed, to give that affent to

every

every act which fhall be laid before him ;
fo more particularly to the act for the fecurity of the kingdom, which has already
paffed this houfe : an act that preferves us
from anarchy : an act that arms a de-
fencelefs people : an act that has coft the
reprefentatives of this kingdom much time
and labour to frame, and the nation a very
great expence : an act that has paffed by a
great majority : and above all, an act that
contains a caution of the higheft importance for the amendment of our conftitution.   I did not prefume the other day,
immediately after this act was voted, to
defire the royal affent ; I thought it a juft
deference to the high commiffioner, not
to mention it at that time.   Neither would
I now, but only that I may have an opportunity to reprefent to his grace, that as he
who gives readily doubles the gift ; fo his

grace

grace has now in his hands the moft glorious and honourable occafion, that any
perfon of this nation ever had, of making
himfelf acceptable; and his memory for
ever grateful to the people of this kingdom : fince the honour of giving the royal
affent to a law, which lays a lafting foundation for their liberties, has been referved
to him.

X.

MY LORD CHANCELLOR,

ON the day that the act for the fecurity
of the kingdom paffed in this houfe, I did
not prefume to move for the royal affent.
The next day of our meeting, I mentioned it with all imaginable refpect and
deference, for his grace the high commiffioner,

miffioner, and divers honourable perfons
feconded me. If now, after the noble
lord who fpoke laft, I infift upon it, I
think I am no way to be blamed. I fhall
not endeavour to fhew the neceffity of
this act, in which the whole fecurity of
the nation now lies, having fpoken to
that point the other day: but fhall take
occafion to fay fomething concerning the
delay of giving the royal affent to acts
paffed in this houfe; for which I could
never hear a good reafon, except that a
commiffioner was not fufficiently inftructed. But that cannot be the true
reafon at this time, becaufe feveral acts
have lain long for the royal affent: in
particular, that to ratify a former act,
for turning the convention into a parliament, and fencing the claim of right,
which no man doubts his grace is fuffi-

ciently

ciently inftructed to pafs. We muft therefore look elfewhere for the reafon of this delay; and ought to be excufed in doing this; fince fo little regard is had, and fo little fatisfaction given to the re-prefentatives of this nation, who have for more than three months employed them-felves with the greateft affiduity in the fer-vice of their country, and yet have not feen the leaft fruit of their labours crowned with the royal affent. Only one act has been touched, for recognizing her majefty's juft right, which is a thing of courfe. This gives but too good reafon to thofe who fpeak freely, to fay that the royal affent is induftrioufly fufpended, in order to oblige fome men to vote, as fhall be moft expedient to a certain intereft; and that this feffion of parliament is continued fo long, chiefly to make men uneafy, who

have-

have neither places nor penfions to bear
their charges; that by this means acts
for money, importation of French wine,
and the like, may pafs in a thin houfe,
which will not fail immediately to receive the royal affent, whilft the acts that
concern the welfare, and perhaps the
very being of the nation, remain un-
touched.

XI.

MY LORD CHANCELLOR,

BEING under fome apprehenfions that
her majefty may receive ill advice in this
affair, from minifters who frequently mif-
take former bad practices for good pre-
cedents, I defire that the third act of the
firft feffion of the firft parliament of king
Charles the Second may be read.

Act

Act the third of the first session, Par. I.
Car. II.

Act asserting his majesty's royal prerogative,
in calling and dissolving of parliaments,
and making of laws.

'THE estates of parliament, now con-
' vened by his majesty's special authority,
' considering that the quietness, stability,
' and happiness of the people, do depend
' upon the safety of the king's majesty's
' sacred person, and the maintenance of
' his sovereign authority, princely power,
' and prerogative royal; and conceiving
' themselves obliged in conscience, and
' in discharge of their duties to almighty
' God, to the king's majesty, and to their
' native country, to make a due acknow-
' ledgment thereof at this time, do there-
' fore unanimously declare, that they will,
                                        ' with

' with their lives and fortunes, maintain
' and defend the fame. And they do
' hereby acknowledge, that the power of
' calling, holding, proroguing, and dif-
' solving of parliaments, and all conven-
' tions and meetings of the eftates does
' folely refide in the king's majefty, his
' heirs and fucceffors. And that as no
' parliament can be lawfully kept, without
' the fpecial warrant and prefence of the
' king's majefty, or his commiffioner;
' fo no acts, fentences or ftatutes, to be
' paffed in parliament, can be binding
' upon the people, or have the authority
' and force of laws, without the fpecial
' authority and approbation of the king's
' majefty, or his commiffioner interponed
' thereto, at the making thereof. And
' therefore the king's majefty, with ad-
' vice and confent of his eftates of parlia-
                       ' ment,

' ment, doth hereby refcind and annul all
' laws, acts, ftatutes, or practices that have
' been, or upon any pretext whatfoever
' may be, or feem contrary to, or incon-
' fiftent with, his majefty's juft power
' and prerogative above-mentioned; and
' declares the fame to have been unlaw-
' ful, and to be void and null in all
' time coming. And to the end that
' this act and acknowledgment, which
' the eftates of parliament, from the fenfe
' of their humble duty and certain know-
' ledge, have hereby made, may receive
' the more exact obedience in time coming;
' it is by his majefty, with advice afore-
' faid, ftatute and ordained, that the punc-
' tual obfervance thereof be fpecially re-
' garded by all his majefty's fubjects, and
' that none of them, upon any pretext
' whatfoever, offer to call in queftion, im-

pugn,

' pugn, or do any deed to the contrary
' hereof, under pain of treafon.'

. MY LORD CHANCELLOR,

THE queftions concerning the king's
prerogative and the people's privileges are
nice and difficult.   Mr. William Colvin,
who was one of the wifeft men this nation ever had, ufed to fay concerning de-
fenfive arms, that he wifhed all princes
thought them lawful, and the people un-
lawful.   And indeed I heartily wifh, that
fomething like thefe moderate fentiments '
might always determine all matters in
queftion between both.   By the conftitution of this kingdom, no act of the
eftates had the force of a law, unlefs
touched by the king's fceptre, which was
his undoubted prerogative.   The touch of
his fceptre gave authority to our laws, as

                              his

his ſtamp did a currency to our coin : but he had no right to refuſe or with-hold either. It is pretended by ſome men, that, in virtue of this act, the king may refuſe the royal aſſent to acts paſſed by the eſtates of the kingdom.   But it ought to be conſidered, that this law is only an acknowledgment and declaration of the king's prerogative, and conſequently gives nothing new to the prince.   The act acknowledges this to be the prerogative of the king, that whatever is paſſed in this houſe, cannot have the force of a law without the royal aſſent, and makes it high treaſon to queſtion this prerogative; becauſe the parliament, during the civil war, had uſurped a power of impoſing their own votes upon the people for law, though neither the king, nor any perſon commiſſionated by him were preſent : and

N   this

this new law was wholly and fimply directed to abolifh and refcind that ufurpa-
tion, as appears by the tenour and exprefs
words of the act; which does neither acknowledge nor declare, that the prince
has a' power to refufe the royal affent to
any act prefented by the parliament. If
any one fhould fay, that the lawgivers
defigned no lefs, and that the principal
contrivers and promoters of the act frequently boafted they had obtained the
negative, as they call it, for the crown; I
defire to know how they will make that
appear, fince no words are to be found in
the act, that fhew any fuch defign; efpecially if we confider that this law was
made by a parliament that fpoke the moft
plainly, leaft equivocally, and moft fully
of all others concerning the prerogative.
And if thofe who promoted the paffing of

this

this act were under so strong a delusion, to think they had obtained a new and great prerogative to the crown by a declaratory law, in which there is not one word to that purpose, it was the hand of Heaven that defeated their design of destroying the liberty of their country.   I know our princes have refused their assent to some acts since the making of this law: but a practice introduced in arbitrary times can deserve no consideration. For my own part, I am far from pushing things to extremity on either hand: I heartily enter into the sentiments of the wise man I mentioned before, and think the people of this nation might have been happy in mistaking the meaning of this law, if such men, as have had the greatest credit with our princes, would have let them into the true sense of it. And therefore those,

N 2

who

who have the honour to advife her majefty, fhould beware of inducing her to a
refufal of the royal affent to the act for
the fecurity of the kingdom, becaufe the
unwarrantable cuftom of rejecting acts
was introduced in arbitrary times.

***

XII.

MY LORD CHANCELLOR,

IT is often faid in this houfe, that parliaments, and efpecially long feffions of
parliament, are a heavy tax and burden
to this nation: I fuppofe they mean as
things are ufually managed: otherwife I
fhould think it a great reflection on the
wifdom of the nation, and a maxim very
pernicious to our government. But indeed in the prefent ftate of things, they
are a very great burden to us. Our parliament

liament feldom meets in winter, when the feafon of the year, and our own private affairs, bring us to town. We are called together for the moft part in fummer, when our country bufinefs, and the goodnefs of the feafon, make us live in town with regret. Our parliaments are fitting both in feed time and harveft, and we are made to toil the whole year. We meet one day in three; though no reafon can be given why we fhould not meet every day, unlefs fuch a one as I am unwilling to name, left thereby occafion fhould be taken to mention it elfewhere to the reproach of the nation. The expences of our commiffioners are now become greater than thofe of our kings formerly were: and a great part of this money is laid out upon equipage, and other things of foreign manufacture, to the great damage of the king-

N 3

dom.

dom. We meet in this place in the after-
noon, after a great dinner, which I think
is not the time of doing bufinefs; and are
in fuch confufion after the candles are
lighted, that very often the debate of one
fingle-point cannot be finifhed; but muft
be put off to another day. Parliaments
are forced to fubmit to the conveniences
of the lords of the feffion, and meetings
of the boroughs; though no good reafon
can be given, why either a lord of the
feffion, or any one deputed to the meetings of the boroughs, fhould be a member
of this houfe; but, on the contrary, experience has taught us the inconvenience
of both. When members of parliament,
to perform the duty they owe to their
country, have left the moft important affairs, and quitted their friends many times
in the utmoft extremity, to be prefent at

this

this place, they are told they may return again; as we were the other day called together only in order to be difmiffed. We have been for feveral days adjourned in this time of harveft, when we had the moft important affairs under deliberation; that as well thofe, who have neither place nor penfion, might grow weary of their attendance, as thofe whofe ill ftate of health makes the fervice of their country as dangerous, though no lefs honourable than if they ferved in the field. Do not thefe things fhew us the neceffity of thofe limitations I had the honour to offer to this houfe? and particularly of that for lodging the power of adjournments in the parliament; that for meetings of parliament to be in winter; that for impowering the prefident to give the royal affent, and afcertaining his falary; with that for ex-

N 4   cluding

cluding all lords of the feffion from being members of parliament? Could one imagine that in this parliament, in which we have had the firft opportunity of amending our conftitution by new conditions of government, occafion fhould be given by reiterating former abufes, to convince all men of the neceffity of farther limitations upon a fucceffor? Or is not this rather to be attributed to a peculiar providence, that thofe who are the great oppofers of limitations, fhould, by their conduct, give the beft reafon for them? But I hope no member of this houfe will be difcouraged either by delay or oppofition; becaufe the liberties of a people are not to be maintained without paffing through great difficulties, and that no toil and labours ought to be declined to preferve a nation from flavery.

XIII.

XIII.

My Lord Chancellor,

I HAVE waited long and with great patience for the refult of this feffion, to fee if I could difcover a real and fincere intention in the members of this houfe, to reftore the freedom of our country in this great and, perhaps, only opportunity. I know there are many different views among us, and all men pretend the good of the nation. But every man here is obliged carefully to examine the things before us, and to act according to his knowledge and confcience, without regard to the views of other men, whatever charity he may have for them: I fay, every man in this place is obliged, by the

oath

oath he has taken, to give such advice as he thinks moſt expedient for the good of his country. The principal buſineſs of this ſeſſion has been the forming of an act for the ſecurity of the kingdom, upon the expiration of the preſent entail of the crown. And though one would have thought, that the moſt eſſential thing which could have entered into ſuch an act, had been to aſcertain the conditions on which the nation would receive a ſucceſſor, yet this has been entirely waved and over-ruled by the houſe. Only there is a caution inſerted in the act, that the ſucceſſor ſhall not be the ſame perſon who is to ſucceed in England, unleſs ſuch conditions of government be firſt enacted, as may ſecure the freedom of this nation, But this is a general and indefinite clauſe, and liable to the dangerous inconveniency of being declared to be fulfilled by giving us two or three inconfiderable laws. So that this feffion of parliament, in which we have had fo great an opportunity of making ourfelves for ever a free people, is like to terminate without any real fecurity for our liberties, or any effential amendant of our conftitution. And now, when we ought to come to particulars, and enact fuch limitations as may fully fatisfy the general claufe, we muft amufe ourfelves with things of little fignificancy, and hardly mention any limitation of moment or confequence. But inftead of this, acts are brought in for regulations to take place during the life of the queen, which we are not to expect, and quite draw us off from the bufinefs we fhould attend. By thefe methods divers well-meaning men have been deluded, whilft others

have

have propofed a prefent nomination of a fucceffor under limitations. But I fear the far greater part have defigned to make their court either to her majefty, the houfe of Hanover, or thofe of St. Germains, by maintaining the prerogative in Scotland as high as ever, to the perpetual enflaving of this nation to the minifters of England. Therefore I, who have never made court to any prince, and I hope never fhall, at the rate of the leaft prejudice to my country, think myfelf obliged, in difcharge of my confcience, and the duty of my oath in parliament, to offer fuch limitations as may anfwer the general claufe in the act for the fecurity of the kingdom. And this I do in two draughts, the one containing the limitations by themfelves; the other with the fame limitations, and a blank for inferting the name

of

of a succeffor. If the houfe fhall think fit to take into confideration that draught which has no blank, and enact the limitations, I fhall reft fatisfied, being as little fond of naming a succeffor as any man. Otherwife, I offer the draught with a blank; to the end that every man may make his court to the perfon he moft affects; and hope by this means to pleafe all parties: the court, in offering them an opportunity to name the succeffor of England, a thing fo acceptable to her majefty and that nation: thofe who may favour the court of St. Germains, by giving them a chance for their pretenfions; and every true Scotfman, in vindicating the liberty of this nation, whoever be the succeffor.

FIRST

FIRST DRAUGHT.

' Our sovereign lady, with advice and
' confent of the eftates of parliament, fta-
' tutes and ordains, that after the deceafe
' of her majefty, whom God long pre-
' ferve, and failing heirs of her body, no
' one fhall fucceed to the crown of this
' realm that is likewife fucceffor to the
' crown of England, but under the limi-
' tations following, which, together with
' the oath of coronation and claim of
' right, they fhall fwear to obferve. That
' all places and offices, both civil and mili-
' tary, and all penfions formerly conferred
' by our kings, fhall ever after be given
' by parliament.—That a new parliament
' fhall be chofen every Michaelmas head-

' court,

' court, to fit the firft of November there-
' after, and adjourn themfelves from time
' to time till next Michaelmas; and that
' they choofe their own prefident.—That a
' committee of thirty-fix members, chofen
' by and out of the whole parliament,
' without diftinction of eftates, fhall, dur-
' ing the intervals of parliament, under the
' king, have the adminiftration of the
' government, be his council, and account-
' able to parliament; with power, in ex-
' traordinary occafions, to call the parlia-
' ment together.'

SECOND DRAUGHT.

' OUR fovereign lady, with advice and
' confent of the eftates of parliament, fta-
' tutes and ordains, that after the deceafe

' of

' of her majesty, whom God long pre-
' serve, and heirs of her body failing,
'   shall succeed to the
' crown of this realm.   But that in case
' the said successor be likewise the suc-
' cessor to the crown of England, the
' said successor shall be under the limita-
' tions following,' &c.

No man can be an enemy to these limitations, in case we have the same king
with England, except he who is so shame-
less a partisan either of the court at St.
Germains, or the house of Hanover, that
he would rather see Scotland continue to
depend upon an English ministry, than
that their prerogative should be any way
lessened in this kingdom.   As for those
who have St. Germains in their view, and
are accounted the highest of all the pre-
                                        rogative-

rogative-men, I would afk them, if we fhould affift them in advancing their prince to the throne of Great Britain, are we, for our reward, to continue ftill in our former dependence on the Englifh court? Thefe limitations are the only teft to difcover a lover of his country from a courtier either to her majefty, Hanover, or St. Germains. For prerogative men, who are for enflaving this nation to the directions of another court, are courtiers to any fucceffor; and let them pretend what they will, if their principles lead neceffarily to fubject this nation to another, are enemies to the nation. Thefe men are fo abfurd as to provoke England, and yet refolve to continue flaves of that court. This country muft be made a field of blood, in order to advance a papift to the throne of Britain. If we fail, we fhall be flaves by right of

O   conqueft,

conqueſt; if we prevail, have the happi-
neſs to continue in our former ſlaviſh dependence. And though to break this yoke,
all good men would venture their all, yet
I believe few will be willing to lie at the
mercy of France and popery, and at the
ſame time draw upon themſelves the indignation and power of England, for the
ſake only of meaſuring our ſtrength with
a much more powerful nation; and to be
ſure to continue ſtill under our former dependence, though we ſhould happen to
prevail. Now, of thoſe who are for the
ſame ſucceſſor with England, I would aſk,
if in that caſe we are not alſo to continue
in our former dependence; which will not
fail always to grow from bad to worſe,
and at length become more intolerable to
all honeſt men, than death itſelf. For my
own part, I think, that even the moſt

zealous

zealous proteftant in the nation, if he have a true regard for his country, ought rather to wifh, were it confiftent with our claim of right, that a papift fhould fucceed to the throne of Great Britain, under fuch limitations as would render this nation free and independent, than the moft proteftant and beft prince, without any. If we may live free, I little value who is king: it is indifferent to me, provided the limitations be enacted, to name or not name; Hanover, St Germains, or whom you will.

XIV.

My Lord Chancellor,

HIS grace, the high commiffioner, having acquainted this houfe, that he has inftructions from her majefty, to give the

royal

royal affent to all acts paffed in this feffion, except that for the fecurity of the king-dom, it will be highly neceffary to provide fome new laws for fecuring our liberty upon the expiration of the prefent entail of the crown. And therefore I fhall fpeak to the firft article of the limitations contained in the fhort act I offered the other day; not only becaufe it is the firft in order, but becaufe I perfuade myfelf you all know that parliaments were formerly chofen annually; that they had the power of appointing the times of their meetings and adjournments, together with the nomination of committees to fuperintend the adminiftration of the government during the intervals of parliament: all which, if it were neceffary, might be proved by a great number of public acts. So that if I demonftrate the ufe and ne-

ceffity

ceffity of the firft article, there will remain no great difficulty concerning the
reft.

My Lord Chancellor,

THE condition of a people, however
unhappy, if they not only know the caufe
of their mifery, but have alfo the remedy
in their power, and yet fhould refufe to
apply it, one would think, were not to be
pitied. And though the condition of good
men, who are concluded and oppreffed by
a majority of the bad, is much to be la-
mented ; yet chriftianity teaches us to fhew
a greater meafure of compaffion to thofe
who are knowingly and voluntarily obfti-
nate to ruin both themfelves and others.
But the regret of every wife and good
man muft needs be extraordinary, when
he fees the liberty and happinefs of his

O 3

country

country not only obstructed, but utterly extinguished by the private and transitory interest of self-designing men, who indeed very often meet their own ruin, but most certainly bring destruction upon their posterity by such courses. Sure, if a man who is intrusted by others, should, for his own private advantage, betray that trust, to the perpetual and irrecoverable ruin of those who trusted him, the liveliest sense and deepest remorse for so great guilt, will undoubtedly seize and terrify the conscience of such a man, as often as the treacherous part he has acted shall recur to his thoughts; which will most frequently happen in the times of his distress, and the nearer he approaches to a life in which those remorses are perpetual. But I hope every man in this house has so well considered these things, as to preserve

him

him from falling into fuch terrible circumftances: and (as all men are fubject
to great failings) if any perfon, placed in
this moft eminent truft, is confcious to
himfelf of having ever been wanting in
duty to his country, I doubt not he will
this day, in this weighty matter, atone for
all, and not blindly follow the opinion
of other men, becaufe he alone muft account for his own actions to his grea
Lord and Mafter.

The limitation, to which I am about
to fpeak, requires, that all places, offices,
and penfions, which have been formerly
given by our kings, fhall, after her majefty
and heirs of her body, be conferred by
parliament, fo long as we are under the
fame prince with England. Without this
limitation, our poverty and fubjection to
the court of England will every day in-

O 4   creafe;

creafe; and the queftion we have now before us is, whether we will be freemen or
flaves for ever? whether we will continue
to depend, or break the yoke of our dependence? and whether we will choofe to
live poor and miferable, or rich, free, and
happy? Let no man think to object, that
this limitation takes away the whole power
of the prince.   For the fame condition of
government is found in one of the moft
abfolute monarchies of the world.   I have
very good authority for what I fay, from
all the beft authors that have treated of the
government of China; but fhall only cite
the words of an able minifter of ftate,
who had very well confidered whatever
had been written on that fubject; I mean
Sir William Temple, who fays, ' That for
' the government, it is abfolute monarchy,
' there being no other laws in China,

                                        ' but

'but the king's orders and commands;
'and it is likewife hereditary, ftill de-
'fcending to the next of blood.   But all
'orders and commands of the king pro-
'ceed through his councils; and are made
'upon the recommendation or petition of
'the council proper and appointed for that
'affair: fo that all matters are debated, de-
'termined, and concluded by the feveral
'councils; and then upon their advices
'and requefts made to the king, they are
'ratified and figned by him, and fo pafs
'into laws.   All great offices of ftate are
'likewife conferred by the king, upon the
'fame recommendations or petitions of
'his feveral councils; fo that none are
'preferred by the humour of the prince
'himfelf, nor by favour of any minifter,
'by flattery or corruption, but by the
'force or appearance of merit, of learn-
'ing,

' ing, and of virtue; which obferved by
' the feveral councils, gain their recom-
' mendations or petitions to the king.'
Thefe are the exprefs words of that minifter. And if under the greateft abfolute
monarchy of the world, in a country
where the prince actually refides; if among
heathens this be accounted a neceffary part
of government for the encouragement of
virtue, fhall it be denied to Chriftians living under a prince who refides in another
nation? Shall it be denied to a people,
who have a right to liberty, and yet are
not capable of any in their prefent circumftances without this limitation? But we
have formed to ourfelves fuch extravagant notions of government, that even in
a limited monarchy nothing will pleafe,
which in the leaft deviates from the model
of France, and every thing elfe muft ftand

3

branded

branded with the name of commonwealth. Yet a great and wife people found this very condition of government neceffary to fupport even an abfolute monarchy. If any man fay, that the empire of China contains divers kingdoms; and that the care of the emperor, and his knowledge of particular men, cannot extend to all: I anfwer, the cafe is the fame with us; and it feems as if that wife people defigned this conftitution for a remedy to the like inconveniences with thofe we labour under at this time.

This limitation will undoubtedly enrich the nation, by ftopping that perpetual iffue of money to England, which has reduced this country to extreme poverty. This limitation does not flatter us with the hopes of riches by an uncertain project; does not require fo much as the condition

dition of our own induſtry; but, by ſaving great ſums to the country, will every year furniſh a ſtock ſufficient to carry on a conſiderable trade, or to eſtabliſh ſome uſeful manufacture at home, with the higheſt probability of ſuccefs: becauſe our miniſters, by this rule of government, would be freed from the influence of Engliſh councils; and our trade be entirely in our own hands, and not under the power of the court, as it was in the affair of Darien. If we do not obtain this limitation, our attendance at London will continue to drain this nation of all thoſe ſums which ſhould be a ſtock for trade. Beſides, by frequenting that court, we not only ſpend our money, but learn the expenſive modes and ways of living, of a rich and luxurious nation: we lay out yearly great ſums in furniture and equi-

page,

page, to the unfpeakable prejudice of the trade and manufactures of our own country. Not that I think it amifs to travel into England, in order to fee and learn their induftry in trade and hufbandry. But at court what can we learn, except a horrid corruption of manners, and an expenfive way of living, that we may for ever after be both poor and profligate?

This limitation will fecure to us our freedom and independence. It has been often faid in this houfe, that our princes are captives in England; and inded one would not wonder if, when our intereft happens to be different from that of England, our kings, who muft be fupported by the riches and power of that nation in all their undertakings, fhould prefer an Englifh intereft before that of this country. It is yet lefs- ftrange, that

English

Englifh minifters fhould advife and procure the advancement of fuch perfons to
the miniftry of Scotland, as will comply
with their meafures and the king's orders;
and to furmount the difficulties they may
meet with from a true Scots intereft,
that places and penfions fhould be be-
ftowed upon parliament-men and others:
I fay, thefe things are fo far from wonder,
that they are inevitable in the prefent
ftate of our affairs. But I hope they
likewife fhew us, that we ought not to
continue any longer in this condition.
Now, this limitation is advantageous to
all. The prince will no more be put
upon the hardfhip of deciding between
an Englifh and a Scots intereft; or the
difficulty of reconciling what he owes
to each nation, in confequence of his
coronation oath. Even Englifh minifters

will

will no longer lie under the temptation of meddling in Scots affairs: nor the minifters of this kingdom, together with all thofe who have places and penfions, be any more fubject to the worft of all flavery. But if the influences I mentioned before fhall ftill continue, what will any other limitation avail us? What fhall we be the better for our act concerning the power of war and peace? fince, by the force of an Englifh intereft and influence, we cannot fail of being engaged in every war, and neglected in every peace.

By this limitation, our parliament will become the moft uncorrupted fenate of all Europe. No man will be tempted to vote againft the intereft of his country, when his country fhall have all the bribes in her own hands; offices, places, penfions. It

will

will be no longer neceffary to lofe one
half of the public cuftoms, that parliament-men may be made collectors. We
will not defire to exclude the officers of
ftate from fitting in this houfe, when the
country fhall have the nomination of them;
and our parliaments, free from corruption,
cannot fail to redrefs all our grievances.
We fhall then have no caufe to fear a refufal of the royal affent to our acts; for
we fhall have no evil counfellor, nor
enemy of his country, to advife it. When
this condition of government fhall take
place, the royal affent will be the ornament of the prince, and never be refufed
to the defires of the people. A general
unanimity will be found in this houfe,
in every part of the government, and
among all ranks and conditions of men.
The diftinctions of court and country

party fhall no more be heard in this nation; nor fhall the prince and people
any longer have a different intereft. Rewards and punifhments will be in the
hands of thofe who live among us, and
confequently beft know the merit of men;
by which means, virtue will be recom-
penfed, and vice difcouraged, and the
reign and government of the prince will
flourifh in peace and juftice.

I fhould never make an end, if I fhould
profecute all the great advantages of this
limitation; which, like a divine influence,
turns all to good, as the want of it has
hitherto poifoned every thing, and brought
all to ruin. I fhall therefore only add
one particular more, in which it will be
of the higheft advantage to this nation.
We all know, that the only way of enflaving a people is by keeping up a ftand-

ing army; that by standing forces all
limited monarchies have been destroyed;
without them none; that so long as any
standing forces are allowed in a nation,
pretexts will never be wanting to increase
them; that princes have never suffered
militias to be put upon any good foot,
left standing forces should appear unne-
cessary. We also know that a good and
well-regulated militia is of so great importance to a nation, as to be the principal
part of the constitution of any free government. Now, by this limitation, the nation will have a sufficient power to render
their militia good and effectual, by the
nomination of officers: and if we would
send a certain proportion of our militia
abroad yearly, and relieve them from time
to time, we may make them as good as
those of Switzerland are; and much more

able

able to defend the country, than any unactive ſtanding forces can be. We may ſave every year great ſums of money, which are now expended to maintain a ſtanding army, and, which is yet more, run no hazard of loſing our liberty by them. We may employ a greater number of officers in thoſe detachments, than we do at preſent in all our forces both at home and abroad; and make better conditions for them in thoſe countries that need their aſſiſtance. For being freed from the influences of Engliſh councils, we ſhall certainly look better than we have hitherto done to the terms on which we may ſend them into the armies either of England or Holland; and not permit them to be abuſed ſo many different ways, as, to the great reproach of the nation, they have been, in their rank, pay, cloth-

ing,

ing, arrears, levy-money, quarters, tranf-
port-fhips, and gratuities.

Having thus fhewn fome of the great
advantages this limitation will bring to
the nation (to which every one of you
will be able to add many more); that it
is not only confiftent with monarchy,
but even with an abfolute monarchy:
having demonftrated the neceffity of fuch
a condition in all empires, which contain
feveral kingdoms; and that without it
we muft for ever continue in a dependence upon the court of England; in the
name of God, what hinders us from em-
bracing fo great a bleffing? Is it becaufe
her majefty will refufe the royal affent
to this act? If fhe do, fure I am, fuch a
refufal muft proceed from the advice of
Englifh counfellors; and will not that
be a demonftration to us, that after her
                              majefty,

majefty, and heirs of her body, we muft
not, cannot any longer continue under
the fame prince with England? Shall we
be wanting to ourfelves? Can her majefty
give her affent to this limitation upon a
fucceffor before you offer it to her? Is
fhe at liberty to give us fatisfaction in
this point, till we have declared to England, by a vote of this houfe, that unlefs
we obtain this condition, we will not
name the fucceffor with them? And then
will not her majefty, even by Englifh
advice, be perfuaded to give her affent;
unlefs her counfellors fhall think fit to
incur the heavy imputation, and run the
dangerous rifk, of dividing thefe nations
for ever? If therefore either reafon, honour, or confcience, have any influence
upon us; if we have any regard either
to ourfelves or pofterity; if there be any

P 3   fuch

such thing as virtue, happiness, or reputation in this world, or felicity in a future state, let me adjure you by all these not to draw upon your heads everlasting infamy, attended with the eternal reproaches and anguish of an evil conscience, by making yourselves and your posterity miserable.

ESSAY

ON THE

GENIUS, CHARACTER, AND WRITINGS

OF

JAMES THOMSON

THE POET.

Intended as a Bafis for writing properly the Life of
that truly excellent Man.

By DAVID STUART, EARL of BUCHAN.

To the Shade of Thomfon.

If Britain, palfied, cannot feel thefe lays
Warm in the heart, and burfting forth thy praife,
Me from Bœotia let the fates convey,
Or death remove me to a brighter day;
To fcenes exalted, where the noble fouls
Of men like thee no fervile court controuls;
Scenes where the good no modeft worth conceals,
And where no praife the worthlefs coxcomb fteals!

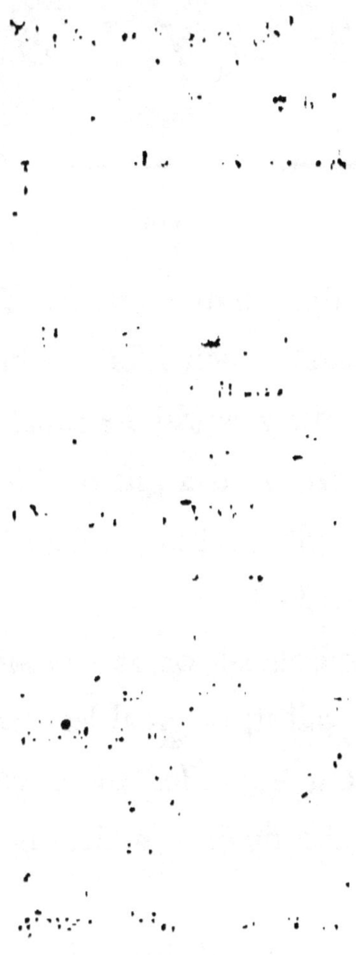

POETRY, that divine energy (for I cannot call it art) which lifts the man of clay from the dirty world he inhabits to the regions of fancy, is a gift of Heaven, and, like all her gifts, is inimitable, and difficult to be defcribed.

In the philofophical, or as I would rather choofe to call it, original language of the Greeks, it is expreffed by a vocable defcriptive of its power, which is creation.

In the Gothic, and all its derivatives in all languages approaching to originality, the name is fynonymous. In old Englifh

and

and Scottifh it is called *making*, and poets were denominated makers.

It is my purpofe in the following Eſſay to honour and defcribe the chief maker of Scotland; to fhew the fuperiority of his genius, to do juftice to his character as a man, and to illuftrate his merit as an author, by exhibiting examples of them all.

I fhall begin with a quotation from Samuel Johnfon's Preface to Thomfon's Poems, becaufe it is well expreffed, and will furnifh a good text for illuftrating the genius of the poet; though it is evident from Johnfon's verfes, that he himfelf was very far from being a maker.

In the counterpoint (as I may call it) of poetry he was a mafter; but of the grounds and melodies he was incapable.

What

What then is *taſte*, but the internal powers
Active, and ſtrong, and feelingly alive
To each fine impulſe ? a diſcerning ſenſe
Of decent and ſublime, with quick diſguſt
From things deform'd, or diſarranged, or groſs
In ſpecies ? This, nor gems, nor ſtores of gold,
Nor purple ſtate, *nor culture* can beſtow;
But God alone, when firſt his active hand
Imprints the ſecret bias of the ſoul.

Pleaſures of the Imag. b. iii. v. 515.

" Thomſon's mode of thinking and of expreſſing his thoughts (writes Johnſon) is original. His blank verſe is no more the blank verſe of Milton, or of any other poet, than the rhymes of Prior are the rhymes of Cowley. His numbers, his pauſes, his diction, are of his own growth, without tranſcription, without imitation. He thinks in a peculiar train, and he thinks always as a man of genius; he looks round on nature and on life with the eye which na-ture and on life with the eye which na-

ture

3

ture beftows only on a poet; the eye that diftinguifhes, in every thing prefented to its view, whatever there is on which imagination can delight to be detained, and with a mind that at once compre- hends the vaft, and attends to the minute.

" The reader of the Seafons wonders that he never faw before what Thomfon fhews him, and that he never yet has felt what Thomfon impreffes."

It was emphatically faid by the greateft of men to his audience, when he was explaining the vital principles of holinefs, " He that hath ears to hear, let him hear!" So it is needlefs to mufter up a legion of words to infufe the knowledge of what conftitutes a genuine poet. The genius of a poet will bear witnefs to itfelf. Po- etry is the flower of fentiment, and mufic is its odour; fo that what is faid of the one is proportionably applicable to the other;

other; and Rousseau's description of genius in music will be found equally just
in the one as in the other. " Seek not
to know what is genius; if thou haft it,
thy feelings will tell thee what it is; if
thou haft it not, thou never wilt know
it."—&c.

Yet as the chaste enjoyment of beauty,
and the just perception of the symmetry
and picturesque perfection of nature, is
in the highest degree conducive to the
sense and practice of virtue, it is of high
moment to enquire what kind of culture
is most friendly to the attainment of taste,
which is the handmaid of genius.

May it not be rationally supposed, that,
without any predisposing circumstances
in the bodily frame, a child will receive
the impressions that are most conducive
to that glorious combination of them

6   (which,

(which, when matured to permanent thought, we call genius) in the country, more readily than in towns or villages, where every thing is too complex for their underftanding?

Will not an education lefs artificial, and tending more to fpontaneous contemplation of natural objects, be more favourable to its attainment than the contrary? And would it not be proper to allow children to feed more upon their own thoughts than on the thoughts and inftructions of others?

Would it not be better to have lefs myftery and technical inftitution in infancy and youth, and more natural knowledge and fentiment than we fee exhibited in fchools and private tuition? And laftly, would it not be better to beftow more time in forming philofophers and citizens,

than

than in training up fchoolmafters and milliners?—But here I ftop. Thomfon paffed his infancy and early youth in the picturefque and paftoral country of Tiviotdale in Scotland, which is full of the elements of natural beauty, wood, water, eminence and rock, with intermixture of rich and beautiful meadow. The horifon was bounded by the Cheviot, a land of fong and of heroic achievement; the venerable ruins of Jedburgh, Dryburgh, Kelfo, and Melrofe, were at hand, to add fuitable impreffions to the whole.

His mother had been well educated, was a woman of uncommon fenfibility, and endowed with fublime affections.

He was cherifhed by Sir William Bennet, at Chefters, near Jedburgh, the moft accomplifhed country gentleman in that part of Scotland. Every thing un-

doubtedly

doubtedly confpired to attune the genius
of Thomfon to fentiment and fong.

" He afk'd no more than fimple nature gave,
" He lov'd the mountains, and enjoy'd their ftorms;
" No falfe defires, no pride-created wants
" Difturb'd the peaceful current of his time,
" And through the reftlefs, ever-tortur'd maze
" Of pleafure or ambition, bid it rage."

It is believed that, at Dryburgh, with
Mr. Haliburton, of New-mains, a friend
of his father's, he firft tuned his Doric
rced, to which he alludes in his Autumn :

" Wafh'd lovely from the Tweed (pure parent ftream),
" Whofe paftoral banks firft heard my Doric reed.

Sir Gilbert Elliot of Minto (too), afterwards Lord Juftice Clerk, a man of elegant tafte, was kind to young Thomfon.

Thomfon fent him a copy of the firft
edition of his Seafons, which Sir Gilbert

fhewing

shewing to a relation of the poet's who was gardener at Minto, he took the book, which was finely bound, into his hands, and having turned it round and round, and gazed on it for some time, Sir Gilbert said to him, " Well, David, what do you think of James Thomson now? There's a book that will make him famous all over the world, and his name immortal!" " Indeed, Sir," said David, " that is a grand book! I did not think the lad had had ingenuity enough to have done such a neat piece of handicraft."

Striking example of the effects of situation and culture upon taste and sentiment!

That Thomson's youth was respectable appears from the countenance he

Q   received

received from Meſſrs. Riccalton and Guſt-
hart ; and the continued attentions of the
latter to the children of Mrs. Thomſon
reflect honour upon his memory, and
excite ſentiments in the feeling heart
that deſerve to be meditated and revolved:
and I hope I am not writing for Chineſe
pedlars, with ſteel-yards at their button-
holes, but to men and women who have
ſtill ſomething in them that preceded the
corruption of our commonwealth !

Thomſon, having been encouraged by
Lady Grizel Baillie to try his fortunes
in London, embarked at Leith in the
autumn of the year 1725, bedewed with
the tears of his amiable and affectionate
mother, the heart-felt recollection of which
produced on her death, which happened not
long after, the following unpremeditated

but

but beautiful verſes, which, though not prepared for the preſs, I have given from a copy in the author's own hand-writing.

ON THE DEATH OF HIS MOTHER *.

From an original, in the Poet's own hand-writing, in the collection of the Earl of Buchan.

YE fabled muſes, I your aid diſclaim,
Your airy raptures, and your fancied flame:
'True genuine woe my throbbing breaſt inſpires,
Love prompts my lays, and filial duty fires;
The ſoul ſprings inſtant at the warm deſign,
And the heart dictates every flowing line.
See! where the kindeſt, beſt of mothers lies,
And death has ſhut her ever-weeping eyes;
Has lodg'd at laſt peace in her weary breaſt,
And lull'd her many piercing cares to reſt.
No more the orphan train around her ſtands,
While her full heart upbraids her needy hands!

---

* Elizabeth Trotter, of a genteel family in the neighbourhood of Greenlaw in Berwickſhire.

Q 2

No

No more the widow's lonely fate she feels,

The shock severe that modest want conceals,

Th' oppressor's scourge, the scorn of wealthy pride,

And poverty's unnumber'd ills beside.

For see ! attended by th' angelic throng,

Through yonder worlds of light she glides along,

And claims the well earn'd raptures of the sky.—

Yet fond concern recalls the mother's eye ;

She seeks the helpless orphans left behind ;

So hardly left ! so bitterly resign'd !

Still, still ! is she my soul's divinest theme,

The waking vision, and the wailing dream :

Amid the ruddy sun's enliv'ning blaze

O'er my dark eyes her dewy image plays,

And in the dread dominion of the night

Shines out again the sadly pleasing sight.

'Triumphant virtue all around her darts,

And more than volumes ev'ry look imparts—

Looks, soft, yet awful, melting, yet serene,

Where both the mother and the saint are seen.

But ah ! that night—that torturing night remains ;

May darkness dye it with its deepest stains,

May joy on it forsake her rosy bow'rs,

And screaming sorrow blast its baleful hours,

When

When on the margin of the briny flood *

Chill'd with a fad prefaging damp I ftood,

Took the laft look, ne'er to behold her more,

And mix'd our murmurs with the wavy roar,

Heard the laft words fall from her pious tongue,

Then, wild into the bulging veffel flung,

Which foon, too foon convey'd me from *her* fight.

Dearer than life, and liberty and light!

Why was I then, ye powers, referv'd for this?

Nor funk that moment in the vaft abyfs?

Devour'd at once by the relentlefs wave,

And whelm'd for ever in a wat'ry grave?—

Down, ye wild wifhes of unruly woe!—

I fee her with immortal beauty glow,

The early wrinkle care-contracted gone,

Her tears all wiped, and all her forrows flown;

Th' exalting voice of Heav'n I hear her breathe,

To footh her foul in agonies of death.

I fee her through the manfions bleft above,

And now fhe meets her dear expecting love.

Heart-cheering fight! but yet, alas! o'erfpread

By the damp gloom of Grief's uncheerful fhade,

---

* On the fhore of Leith, when he embarked for
London.

Q 3

Come

Come then of reason the reflecting hour,

And let me trust the kind o'er-ruling Power,

Who from the right commands the shining day,

The poor man's portion, and the orphan's stay!

THOMSON's ELEGY ON THE DEATH OF AIKMAN, THE

PAINTER *.

*From a MS. of the Author's own hand-writing in the
collection of the Earl of Buchan.*

OH could I draw, my friend, thy genuine mind,

Just, as the living forms by thee design'd,

Of Raphael's figures none should fairer shine,

Nor Titian's colours longer last than mine.

A mind

---

* Mr. Aikman died at London, on the 7th of June,
O. S. 1731, from whence his remains were sent to Scotland,
and interred in the Gray-Friars church-yard, close by
those of his only son, who had been buried only a few
months before.

Mr. Aikman was the son of William Aikman of Cairny,
Esq. (sheriff depute of Forfarshire, a lawyer of eminence,

and

A mind in wifdom old, in lenience young,

From fervent truth where every virtue fprung;

Where all was real, modeft, plain, fincere;

Worth above fhow, and goodnefs unfevere:

View'd round and round, as lucid diamonds throw

Still as you turn them a revolving glow;

So did his mind reflect with fecret ray,

In various virtues, heav'n's internal day,

Whether in high difcourfe it foar'd fublime,

And fprung impatient o'er the bounds of Time,

---

and in nomination for a judge's gown at the time of his death) by Margaret, fifter of Sir John Clerk of Pennycuik, Baronet.

He was born on the 24th of October 1682, and was educated by his parents with great care, and deftined for the profeffion of the law. Nature thought fit to deftine and fit him for another more elegant, not lefs liberal, and certainly much more delightful. He went to Italy in the year 1705, and returned to Britain in 1710, not only a good painter, but an accomplifhed and agreeable man.

In the Gothic reigns of George I. and II. he could look for nothing but money for ftarch heads and periwigs, and ftarch heads and periwigs was he forced to delineate and paint till his dying day. O che fciagura!

Or

Or wand'ring nature through with raptur'd eye,

Ador'd the hand that turn'd yon azure ſky:

Whether to ſocial life he bent his thought,

And the right poiſe of mingling paſſions ſought,

Gay converſe bleſs'd; or in the thoughtful grove

Bid the heart open every ſource of love.

New varying lights ſtill ſet before your eyes

The juſt, the good, the ſocial, or the wiſe.

For ſuch a death who can, who would, refuſe

The friend a tear, a verſe the mournful muſe?

Yet pay we juſt acknowledgment to Heaven,

Though ſnatch'd ſo ſoon, that Aikman e'er was

      given.

A friend, when dead, is but remov'd from ſight,

Hid in the luſtre of eternal light :

Oft with the mind he wonted converſe keeps

In the lone walk, or when the body ſleeps

Lets in a wand'ring ray, and all elate

Wings and attraẟs her to another ſtate * ;

And when the parting ſtorms of life are o'er,

May yet rejoin him on a happier ſhore.

---

* This and the three preceding lines are not in the
MS. of Mrs. Forbes Aikman.

As thofe we love decay, we die in part,
String after ftring is fever'd from the heart;
Till loofen'd life at laft—but breathing clay,
Without one pang, is glad to fall away.
Unhappy he who lateft feels the blow,
Whofe eyes have wept o'er ev'ry friend laid low,
Dragg'd ling'ring on from partial death to death,
And dying, all he can refign is breath.

SONG WRITTEN IN HIS EARLY YEARS, AND AFTER-
WARDS SHAPED FOR HIS AMANDA.

From a MS. in the collection of the Earl of Buchan.

FOR ever, Fortune, wilt thou prove
An unrelenting foe to love;
And when we meet a mutual heart,
Come in between and bid us part;
Bid us figh on from day to day,
And wifh and wifh the foul away;
Till youth and genial years are flown,
And all the life of life is gone?
But bufy bufy ftill art thou,
To bind the lovelefs joylefs vow,

The

The heart from pleafure to delude,

And join the gentle to the rude * ;

For pomp, and noife, and fenfelefs fhow,

To make us nature's joys forego,

Beneath a gay dominion groan,

And put the golden fetter on !

To Dr. De la Cour, in Ireland.

On his Profpect of Poetry.

HAIL gently-warbling De la Cour, whofe fame,

Spurning Hibernia's folitary coaft,

Where fmall rewards attend the tuneful throng,

Pervades Britannia's well-difcerning ifle :

In fpite of all the gloomy-minded tribe

That would eclipfe thy fame, ftill fhall the mufe,

High foaring o'er the tall Parnaffian mount

---

  * For once, O Fortune ! hear my prayer,

    And I abfolve thy future care :

    All other bleffings I refign,

    Make but the dear Amanda mine !

The original of this alfo, as prepared for his miftrefs, is in Lord Buchan's poffeffion.

With

With spreading pinions—sing thy wondrous praise,
In strains attun'd to the seraphic lyre.
Sing unappall'd, though mighty be the theme!
O! could she in thy own harmonious strain,
Where softest numbers smoothly flowing glide
In trickling cadence; where the milky maze
Devolves in silence; by the harsher sound
Of hoarser periods still unruffled, could.
Her lines but like thine own Euphrates flow—
Then might she sing in numbers worthy thee.
But what can language do, when Fancy finds
Herself unequal to the lovely task?
Can feeble words thy vivid colours paint,
Or shew the sweets which inexhaustive flow?
Hearken ye woods, and long-resounding groves;
Listen ye streams, soft purling thro' the meads,
And hymning horrid, all ye tempests roar.
Awake, ye woodlands! sing, ye warbling larks,
In wildly luscious notes! But most of all,
Attend, ye grateful fair, attend the youth
Who sweetly sings of nature and of you:
From you alone his conscious breast expects
Its soft rewards, by sordid love of gain
Unbiafs'd, undebas'd; to meaner minds

Belong

Belong fuch narrow views; his nobler foul,
Tranfported with a gen'rous thirft of fame,
Sublimely rifes with expanded wings,
And through the lucid empyrean foars.
So the young eagle wings its rapid way
Thro' heaven's broad azure; fometimes fprings aloft,
Now drops, now cleaves with even-waving wings
The yielding air, nor feas nor mountains ftop
Its flight impetuous, gazing at the fun
With irretorted eye, whilft he pervades
A tracklefs void, and unexplor'd before.
Long had the curious traveller ftrove to find
The ruins of afpiring Babylon—
In vain—for nought the niceft eye could trace
Save one wide, wat'ry, undiftinguifh'd wafte:
But you with more than magic art have rais'd
Semiramis's city from its grave;
You have revers'd the fcripture curfe, which faid,
Dragons fhall here inhabit; in your page
We view the rifing fpires; the hurried eye
Diftracted wanders through the verdant maze;
In middle air the pendent gardens hang,
Tremendous ceiling!—whilft no folar beam
Falls on the lengthen'd gloom beneath; the woods

Project

Project above a steep-alluring shade;
The finish'd garden opens to the view
Wide-stretching vistas, while the whisp'ring wind.
Dimples along the breezy-ruffled lake.
  Now every tree irregular, and busts
Are prodigal of harmony: the birds
Frequent th' aërial wood, and nature blushes,
Asham'd to find herself outdone by art:
These and a thousand beauties could I sing,
Collecting like the ever-toiling bee
From yonder mingled wilderness of flow'rs
The aromatic sweets; while you, great youth!
O'er thy decaying country chief preside;
Be thou her genius call'd, inspire her youth
With noble emulation to arrive
At Helicon's fair font, which few, alas!
Save you, have tasted of Hibernian youth.
Thy country, tho' corrupted, brought thee forth,
And deem'd her greatest ornament; and now
Regards thee as her brightest northern star.
Long may you reign as such; and should grim Time,
With iron teeth, deprive us of our Pope,
Then we'll transplant thy blooming laurels fresh
From your bleak shore to Albion's happier coast.

Thomson's

Thomson's Letter to Mr. George Rofs *.

London, November 6th, 1736.

DEAR ROSS,

I OWN I have a good deal of affurance, after afking one favour of you, never to anfwer your letter till I afk another. But not to mince the matter, and all apologies apart, hearken to my requeft—My fifters have been advifed by their friends to fet up at Edinburgh a little milliner's fhop; and if you can conveniently advance to them twelve pounds, on my account, it will be a particular favour. That will fet them a-going, and I defign from time to time to fend them goods from hence. My whole account I will pay you when you come up here, not in poetical paper

* From an original in Lord Buchan's collection.

credit,

credit, but in the folid money of this dirty world. I will not draw upon you, in eafe you be not prepared to defend your-felf; but if your purfe be valiant, pleafe to enquire for Jean or Elizabeth Thomfon, at the Reverend Mr. Gufthart's; and if this letter be not a fufficient teftimony of the debt, I will fend you whatever you defire.

It is late, and I would not lofe this poft. Like a laconic man of bufinefs, therefore, I muft here ftop fhort; though I have feveral things to impart to you, and, through your canal, to the deareft, trueft, heartieft youth that treads on Scottifh ground. The next letter I write you fhall be wafhed clean from bufinefs in the Caftalian fountain.

I am whipping and fpurring to finifh a tragedy for you this winter, but am

ftill

ftill at fome diftance from the goal, which makes me fear being diftanced. Remember me to all friends, and above them all to Mr. Forbes. Though my affection to him is not fanned by letters, yet is it as high as when I was his brother in the virtù, and played at chefs with him in a poft-chaife.

I am, dear Rofs,

Moft fincerely and affectionately yours,
JAMES THOMSON.

Thomfon to Mr. George Rofs.

London, Jan. 12, 1737.

DEAR SIR,

HAVING been entirely in the country of late, finifhing my play, I did not receive yours till fome days ago. It was kind in you not *to draw* rafhly upon me, which at prefent had put me into danger:

but

but very foon (that is to fay, about two months hence) I fhall have a golden buckler, and you may draw boldly.—— My play * is received in Drury-lane play-houfe, and will be put into my lord chamberlain's or his deputy's hands to-morrow.—May we hope to fee you this winter, and to have the affiftance of your hands, in cafe it is acted? What will become of you? I am afraid the *creepy* † and you will be acquainted.—Forbes, I hope, is cheerful, and in good health. Shall we never fee him? or fhall I go to him before he comes to us? I long to fee him, in order to play out that game of chefs which we left unfinifhed. Remember me kindly to him, with all the

* Agamemnon.

† Stool, ufed in the Scotch churches for doing penance.

R   zealous

zealous truth of old friendſhip.   Pettie *
came here two or three days ago : I have
not yet feen the round man of God to
be.   He is to be parfonified a few days
hence.—How a gown and caſſock will
become him ! and with what a holy leer
he will edify the devout females ! There
is no doubt of his having a call; for he
is immediately to enter upon a tolerable
living.   God grant him more, and as
fat as himfelf.   It rejoices me to fee one
worthy, honeſt, excellent man raifed, at
leaſt to an independency.   Pray make

* Rev. Mr. Patrick Murdoch, the oily man of
God of the Caſtle of Indolence.

    " A little, round, fat, oily man of God,
    " Was one I chiefly mark'd among the fry;
    " He had a roguiſh twinkle in his eye,
    " And ſhone all glittering with unholy dew,
    " If a tight damſel chaunc'd to trippen by."

my compliments to my Lord Prefident * .
and all friends. I fhall be glad to hear
more at large from you. Juft now I
am with the alderman, who wifhes you
all happinefs, and defires his fervice to
Jock. Believe me to be

Ever moft affectionately yours,
JAMES THOMSON.

---

*Thomfon to Mr. Lyttelton, afterwards
Lord Lyttelton.*

London, July 14th, 1743.

DEAR SIR,

I HAD the pleafure of yours fome
pofts ago, and have delayed anfwering it
hitherto, that I might be able to determine when I could have the happinefs of
waiting upon you.

Hagley is the place in England I moft
defire to fee; I imagine it to be greatly

* Prefident Forbes.

R 2

delightful

delightful in itfelf, and I know it to be fo to the higheft degree by the company it is animated with.

Some reafons prevent my waiting upon you immediately; but if you will be fo good as let me know how long you de- fign to ftay in the country, nothing fhall hinder me from paffing three weeks or a month with you before you leave it. As this will fall in autumn, I fhall like it the better, for I think that feafon of the year the moft pleafing, and the moft poetical. The fpirits are not then diffi- pated with the gaiety of fpring, and the glaring light of fummer, but compofed into a ferious and tempered joy.—The year is perfect. In the mean time I will go on with correcting the Seafons, and hope to carry down more than one of them with me. The mufes, whom you obligingly fay I fhall bring along with me, me, I shall find with you—the mufes of the great fimple country, not the little fine-lady mufes of Richmond-hill.

I have lived fo long in the noife, or at leaft the diftant din of the town, that I begin to forget what retirement is: with you I shall enjoy it in its higheft elegance, and pureft fimplicity. The mind will not only be foothed into peace, but enlivened into harmony. My compliments attend all at Hagley, and particularly her * who gives it charms to you it never had before.

Believe me to be ever,

With the greateft refpect,

Moft affectionately yours,

JAMES THOMSON.

* Lucy Fortefcue, daughter of Hugh Fortefcue, Efq. of Filleigh, in the county of Devon, married

                                                       to

Thomſon's Letter to his Siſter, Mrs. Jean Thomſon, at Lanark.

Hagley, in Worceſterſhire,

October 4th, 1747.

MY DEAR SISTER,

I THOUGHT you had known me better than to interpret my ſilence into a

decay

to Mr. Lyttelton in the year 1742, whoſe amiable qualities, exemplary conduct, and uniform practice of religion and virtue, rendered her the delight and regret of all her acquaintance. She died in the beginning of the year 1746, in the 29th year of her age, leaving her huſband one ſon, Thomas, the late Lord Lyttelton, and a daughter, Lucy, married in the year 1765 to Lord Valentia. Who has not ſeen and wept over the beautiful monody conſe-crated to her memory by the good Lord Lyttelton? If there is a living ſoul that has read it without emotion, I envy not their condition upon a throne.

It

decay of affection, efpecially as your be-
haviour has always been fuch as rather to
increafe than to diminifh it.   Don't imagine, becaufe I am a bad correfpondent,
that I can ever prove an unkind friend and
brother.   I muft do myfelf the juftice to

It is full of every thing that gives dignity to man.
Her epitaph at Hagley is lefs known.—

" Made to engage all hearts, and charm all eyes,
" Tho' meek, magnanimous; tho' witty, wife:
" Polite, as all her life in courts had been;
" Yet good, as fhe the world had never feen:
" The noble fire of an exalted mind
" With gentleft female tendernefs combin'd.
" Her fpeech was the melodious voice of love;
" Her fong, the warbling of the vernal grove;
" Her eloquence was fweeter than her fong,
" Soft as her heart, and as her reafon ftrong.
" Her form each beauty of her mind exprefs'd;
" Her mind was virtue, by the Graces drefs'd.

tell

R 4

tell you, that my affections are naturally very fixed and conſtant; and if I had ever reaſon of complaint againſt you (of which, by the bye, I have not the leaſt ſhadow), I am conſcious of ſo many defects in myſelf, as diſpoſe me to be not a little charitable and forgiving.

It gives me the trueſt heartfelt ſatiſfaction to hear you have a good kind huſband, and are in eaſy contented circumſtances: but were they otherwiſe, that would only awaken and heighten my tenderneſs towards you. As our good and tender-hearted parents did not live to receive any material teſtimonies of that higheſt human gratitude I owed them (than which nothing could have given me more pleaſure), the only return I can make them now, is by kindneſs to thoſe

they

they left behind them. Would to God poor Lizzy* had lived longer, to be a farther witnefs of the truth of what I fay, and that I might have had the pleafure of feeing

---

* Elizabeth, married to Mr. Bell, mother of the prefent Dr. Bell, rector of the parifh of Coldftream, in Berwickfhire, a gentleman who poffeffes much of the worth and genius of his uncle, and who is now employed in preparing a new and collated edition of Thomfon's Works, with a more correct account of his life than has hitherto appeared; in which pious work I have done myfelf the honour to afford fome little affiftance in the collection of materials. To this edition it is propofed to prefix an engraving from the poet's buft in Weftminfter Abbey, and another from the fketch of a monument drawn by Mr. Hicky, which was tranfmitted to the Earl of Buchan by Sir Jofhua Reynolds.

The text of this new edition for the Seafons is intended to be that in 4to. of the year 1730, in which Autumn made its firft appearance: the additions

feeing once more a fifter who fo truly deferved my efteem and love. But fhe is happy, while we muft toil a little longer here below: let us however do it cheerfully and gratefully, fupported by the pleafing hope of meeting yet again on a fafer fhore, where to recollect the ftorms and difficulties of life will not perhaps be inconfiftent with that blifsful ftate. You did right to call your daughter by her name, for you muft needs have had a

tions and alterations to be printed in italics. The following is a ftatement of the additional lines made to the Seafons after that edition:

		lines
To Spring	- -	85
Summer	- -	599
Autumn	- -	96
Winter	- -	188
		968

particular

particular tender friendſhip for one another, endeared as you were by nature, by
having paſſed the affectionate years of your
youth together, and by that great ſoftener
and engager of hearts, mutual hardſhip.
That it was in my power to eaſe it
a little, I account one of the moſt ex-
quiſite pleaſures of my life.—But enough
of this melancholy, though not unpleaſ-
ing ſtrain.

I eſteem you for your ſenſible and
diſintereſted advice to Mr. Bell, as you
will ſee by my letter to him : as I approve
entirely of his marrying again, you may
readily aſk me, why I don't marry at all?
My circumſtances have hitherto been ſo
variable and uncertain in this fluctuating
world, as induce to keep me from engaging in ſuch a ſtate; and now, though
they are more ſettled, and of late (which

you

you will be glad to hear) confiderably improved, I begin to think myfelf too far
advanced in life for fuch youthful undertakings, not to mention fome other petty
reafons that are apt to ftartle the delicacy
of difficult old bachelors. I am, however,
not a little fufpicious, that was I to pay a
vifit to Scotland (which I have fome
thoughts of doing foon), I might poffibly
be tempted to think of a thing not eafily
repaired if done amifs. *I have always
been of opinion, that none make better wives
than the ladies of Scotland ;* and yet who
more forfaken than they, while the gentlemen are continually running abroad all
the world over ? Some of them, it is true,
are wife enough to return for a wife.—
You fee I am beginning to make intereft
already with the Scots ladies. But no
more of this infectious fubject.—Pray let

me hear from you now and then; and though I am not a regular correspondent, yet perhaps I may mend in that respect. Remember me kindly to your husband [*], and believe me to be

Your most affectionate brother,
JAMES THOMSON.

(Addressed) To Mrs. Thomson, in Lanark.

BUT

[*] Mr. Thomson was rector of the grammar school at Lanark, and from him, or Mrs. Thomson, Mr. Boswell obtained a copy of the original of this letter, which original is now in the possession of Mr. James Craig, architect, Thomson's youngest sister's son, who is likewise possessed of copies of Thomson's juvenile poems, of his snuff-box, and seal of arms, which hung at his watch, and of his original portrait painted by Hudson, for Mr. Millar, the bookseller, which was presented to him by Lady Grant, first married to that worthy friend of the

poet's,

BUT the higheſt encomium of Thomſon is to be given him on account of his attachment to the cauſe of political and civil liberty. A free conſtitution of government, or what I would beg leave to call the *autocracy* of the people, is the panacea of moral diſeaſes, and after having been ſought for in vain for ages, has been diſcovered in the boſom of truth, on the right hand of common ſenſe, and at the feet of philoſophy; the printing preſs has been the diſpenſary, and half the world

poet's, and was a daughter of Johnſon, the engraver to the Bank of Scotland.

Lord Buchan preſented to Mr. Craig the plaſter of Paris caſt of the buſt of Thomſon, which was intended to have been crowned on Ednam-Hill, and he gave a ſketch for a monument to the memory of his uncle for that conſpicuous ſituation.

have

have become voluntary patients of this healing remedy.

It is glorious for Thomſon's memory that he ſhould have deſcribed the platform of a perfeﾋ government, as Milton deſcribed the platform of a perfeﾋ garden— the one in the midſt of Gothic inſtitutions of feudal origin, and the other in the midſt of clipped yews and ſpouting lions.

Eighteen years after Thomſon's death the late Lord Chatham agreed with me in making this remark; and when I ſaid, " But, Sir, what will become of poor England, that doats on the imperfeﾋions of her pretended conſtitution?" he replied, " My dear Lord, the gout will diſpoſe of me ſoon enough to prevent me from feeling the conſequences of this infatuation: but before the end of this century either the parliament will reform itſelf from
within,

within, or be reformed with a vengeance
from without." Pythonick fpeech, fpeedily
to be verified !

" Should then the times arrive (which Heaven avert!)
" That Britons bend unnerv'd, not by the force
" Of arms, more generous, and more manly, quell'd,
" But by *corruption's* foul-dejecting arts,
" Arts impudent, and grofs ! by *their own* gold,
" *In part* beftow'd to bribe them to give *all :*
" With party raging, or immers'd in *floth,*
" Should *fhamelefs pens* for fly corruption plead ;
" The hired affaffins of the commonweal !
" That nation fhall another Carthage be."

———————————

Britons ! be firm !—nor let corruption fly
Twine round your hearts indiffoluble chains !
The fteel of Brutus burft the groffer bonds
By Cæfar caft o'er Rome ; but ftill remain'd
The foft enchanting fetters of the mind,
And *other Cæfars* rofe. Determin'd hold
Your INDEPENDANCE ; for, *that* once deftroy'd,

Unfounded,

Unfounded, FREEDOM is a morning dream,
That flits aërial from the spreading eye.

• No wonder that, when the brutal Johnson tried to read liberty when it firſt appeared, he ſoon deſiſted, when Johnſon's
countrymen try to read France's liberty,
and deſiſt !

" Pudet hæc opprobria nobis, et dici potuiſſe,
" Et non potuiſſe refelli !

Though I have not the tranſcendent
honour of being a member of the Britiſh
parliament, let not the powerful deſpiſe
my ſayings—I am the voice of one cry-
ing in the wilderneſs of politics—*Make
ſtraight your ways, for the empire of de-
luſion is at an end.*

S

Thomſon

Thomſon to Mr. Paterſon, of the Leeward Iſlands *.

DEAR PATERSON,

IN the firſt place, and previouſly to my letter, I muſt recommend to your favour and protećtion, Mr. James Smith, ſearcher

---

* Mr. Paterſon, a companion of Thomſon, afterwards his deputy as ſurveyor general of the Leeward Iſlands, and his ſucceſſor in the office, uſed to write out fair copies of his works, ſeveral of which are in my collećtion. This gentleman, as Murdoch informs us, courted the Tragic Muſe, and wrote a piece in that line, with Arminius for its hero.

When he preſented it to the manager of Drury-lane play-houſe, the hand-writing of Edward and Eleonora being immediately recogniſed, it was ſcouted, and he was glad to ſell it for a trifle to a good-natured bookſeller.

Murdoch's Life of Thomſon.

in

in St. Chriſtopher's, and I beg of you, as occaſion ſhall ſerve, and as you find he merits it, to advance him in the buſineſs of the cuſtoms. He is warmly recommended to me by Sargent, who in verity turns out one of the beſt men of our youthful acquaintance, honeſt, honourable, friendly, and generous.—If we are not to oblige one another, life becomes a paltry ſelfiſh affäir, a pitiful morſel in a corner! Sargent is ſo happily married, that I could almoſt ſay, the ſame caſe happen to us all.

That I have not anſwered ſeveral letters of yours, is not owing to the want of friendſhip, and the ſincereſt regard for you ; but you know me well enough to account for my ſilence, without my ſaying any more upon that head ; beſides, I have very little to ſay, that is worthy to

be

be tranfmitted over the great ocean.   The
world either futilifes * fo much, or we
grow fo dead to it, that its tranfactions
make but a feeble impreffion on us.   † Retirement and nature are more and more
my paffion every day; and now, even
now, the charming time comes on:
heaven is juft upon the point, or rather
in the very act, of giving earth a green
gown.   The voice of the nightingale is
heard in our lane ‡.

You

* A verb coined by Thomfon from the adjective
futile.

† On this account it has been fuggefted, that the
moft proper monument for Thomfon would be a
modeft Doric portico, adjoining to a cottage ftored
with the beft books on natural hiftory, to be kept
by fome of the poet's poor relations, with a falary.

‡ The bird-catchers about London generally
obferve the fong of the nightingale in the firft or

fecond

You must know that I have enlarged
my rural domain much to the same di-
menfions you have done yours—the two
fields next to me; from the firft of which
I have walled—no, no,—paled in about
as much as my garden confifted of before;
fo that the walk runs round the hedge,
where you may figure me walking any
time of the day, and fometimes under
night.   For you, I imagine you reclining
under cedars and palmettos, and there
enjoying more magnificent flumbers than
are known to the pale climates of the

fecond week of April. This letter of Thomfon's
having no date, it is impoffible to determine exactly
from circumftances when it was written; but as
the firing began at Maeftricht in the firft week, it
may be gueffed that the letter was written about
the middle of the month, fince he fpeaks in the clofe
of the letter of the news of the fiege being frefh.

S 3

north;

north; flumbers rendered awful and divine, by the folemn ftillnefs and deep fervors of the torrid noon. At other times I imagine you drinking punch in groves of lime or orange trees, gathering pine apples from hedges as commonly as we may blackberries, poetifing under lofty laurels, or making love under full-fpread myrtles.—But to lower my ftyle a little—as I am fuch a genuine lover of gardening, why don't you remember me in that inftance, and fend me fome feeds of things that might fucceed here during the fummer, though they cannot perfect their feeds fufficiently in this, to them, ungenial climate, to propagate?—in the which cafe is the calliloo; that, from the feed it bore here, produced plants puny, rickctty, and good for nothing. There are other things certainly with you, not

yet

yet brought over hither, that might flourifh here in the fummer-time, and live
tolerably well, provided they were fhel-
tered during the winter in a green-houfe.

You will give me no fmall pleafure,
by fending me, from time to time, fome
of thefe feeds, if it were no more than to
amufe me in making the trial *.

* The amufements of Thomfon were chiefly the
contemplation of nature, the ftudy of natural hiftory as a fcience, voyages and travels, and the philofophy of civil hiftory; of which laft he has given
an excellent fpecimen in his Liberty, as he has of
the firft in his Seafons and Caftle of Indolence.
Gardening, except in the ftiff ornamental ftyle of
Holland, had made but little progrefs in England
in the days of Thomfon. There were no Curtifes,
Aytouns, or Forfythes, ftill lefs any Wheatlys or
Walpoles. Philip Miller, the author of the Gardener's Dictionary, was almoft the only man who
could be of ufe to Thomfon in his refearches.

S 4

With

With regard to the brother gardeners, you ought to know, that, as they are half vegetables, the animal part of them will never have fpirit enough to confent to the tranfplanting of the vegetable into diftant dangerous, climates : they, happily for themfelves, have no other idea but to dig on here, eat, drink, fleep, and kifs their wives.

As to more important bufinefs, I have nothing to write to you. You know beft the courfe of it. Be (as you always muft be) juft and honeft; but if you are un-happily romantic, you fhall come home without money, and write a tragedy on yourfelf. Mr. Lyttelton told me that the Grenvilles and he had ftrongly recom-mended the perfon the governor and you propofed for that confiderable office, lately fallen vacant in your department, and that

there

there were good hopes of fucceeding. He told me alfo that Mr. P. had faid it was not to be expected that offices fuch as that is, for which the greateft intereft is made here at home, could be accorded to your recommendation : but that, as to the middling or inferior offices, if there was not fome particular reafon to the contrary, regard would be had thereto. This is all that can be reafonably defired; and if you are not infected with a certain Creolean diftemper (whereof I am perfuaded your foul will utterly refift the contagion, as I hope your body will that of their natural ones), there are few men fo capable of that unperifhable happinefs, that peace and fatisfaction of mind that proceed from being reafonable and moderate in our defires, as you are. Thefe are the treafures, dug from an inexhauftible mine in our own breafts;

which

which, like thofe in the kingdom of heaven, the ruft of time cannot corrupt, nor
thieves break through and fteal. I muft
learn to work at this mine a little more,
being ftruck off from a certain hundred
pounds a year which you know I had.
Weft, Mallet, and I were all routed in one
day. If you would know why—out of
refentment to our friend* in Argyll-ftreet.

Yet

* George, afterwards Lord Lyttelton.—Whether
we contemplate the character of this worthy man in
public or private life, we are juftified in affirming that
he abounded in virtues not only fufficient to create
reverence and efteem, but to excite the affectionate
remembrance of all who had the honour and pleafure of his acquaintance. " His wit was nature by
" the Graces dreft"——

 " His was the large ambitious wifh,
 " To make men bleft; the figh for fuffering worth
 " Loft in obfcurity; the noble fcorn

" Of

Yet I have hopes given me of having it reftored with intereft, fome time or other. Ah ! *that fome time or other is a great deceiver.*   Coriolanus has not yet appeared upon the ftage, from the little dirty jealoufy of Tullus *—I mean of him who was defired to act Tullus—towards him †

" Of tyrant pride; the fearlefs great refolve,
" Th' awaken'd throb for virtue and for fame,
" The fympathies of love and friendfhip dear;
" With all the focial offspring of the heart."

* Garrick.

† Quin.—Thofe who wifh to amufe themfelves with the broils of the theatre may confult Davies's Dramatic Mifcellanies, and his Life of Garrick, for the campaigns (as the theatricals are pleafed to call them) of the winters 47 and 48.—For my own part, I admire the great Frederick of Pruffia, who coming to his concert, and finding the muficians quarrelling, exclaimed with a good-natured fmile—" Arrangez vous, coquins."

who

who can alone act Coriolanus. Indeed, the firft has entirely jockeyed the laft off the ftage for this feafon; but I believe he will return on him next feafon, like a giant in his wrath. Let us have a little more patience, Paterfon; nay, let us be cheerful. At laft all will be well; at leaft all will be over—*here* I mean: God forbid it fhould be hereafter. But as fure as there is a God, that will not be fo*. Now that I am prating of myfelf, know that after fourteen or fifteen years, the Caftle of Indolence comes abroad in a

* It is pleafing to fee the laft expreffions of the poet's confidence, that the form of the foul is eternal; that great fpirits perifh not with the body. There may be worthlefs veffels, and there may be veffels fitted for deftruction; but of all that Heaven has endowed with feelings to enjoy it, nothing fhall be loft, and the King of Heaven fhall raife it up again at the laft day!

2   fort-

fortnight *.   It will certainly travel as far as Barbadoes.   You have an apartment in it, as a night penfioner, which you may remember I filled up for you during our delightful party at North Ham.   Will ever thefe days return again ? Don't you remember your eating the raw fifh that was never caught ? All our friends are

* The Caftle of Indolence is the fineft poem of the kind in any language—worthy of the ripened tafte of Thomfon, and of a polifhed age.

O thou, whofe genius, powerful yet refin'd,
Whofe bard-like virtues, and confummate fkill
To touch the finer fprings that move the heart,
Join'd to whate'er the Graces could beftow,
And all Apollo's animating fire,
Gave thee with pleafing dignity to fhine
At once the friend, the ornament, and joy
Of Phœbus' fons—permit a rural mufe,
Thus in thy words to hail thy honour'd fhade !
Thus to proclaim thee to a downward age
The friend of virtuè, liberty, and love.

pretty

pretty much in ſtatu quo, except it be poor Mr. Lyttelton. He has had the ſevereſt trial an humane tender heart can have *: but the old phyſician Time will at laſt cloſe up his wounds, though there muſt always remain an inward ſmarting. Mitchel † is in the houſe for Aberdeen-ſhire, and has ſpoken modeſtly well: I hope he will be in ſomething elſe ſoon. None deſerves better: true friendſhip and humanity dwell in his heart. Gray is working hard at paſſing his accounts. I ſpoke to him about that affair. If he

* The death of his Lucy.

† Sir Andrew Mitchel of Thainſtoun. Not a word of exaggeration. He was an excellent man. It is. needleſs for me to attempt ſaying any thing about a man who was eſteemed by Frederick the Great, and beloved by his acquaintance and rela-tions.

gives

gives you any trouble about it, even that of dunning, I fhall think of it ftrangely ; but I dare fay he is too friendly to do it. He values himfelf juftly upon being friendly to his old friends, and you are among the oldeft. Symmer is at laft tired of quality, and is going to take a femi-country houfe at Hammerfmith. I am forry that honeft fenfible Warrender (who is in town) feems to be ftunted in church preferment. He ought to be a tall cedar in the houfe of the Lord. If he is not fo at laft, it will add more fuel to my indignation, that burns already too intenfely, and throbs towards an eruption. Peter Murdoch is in town, tutor to Admiral Vernon's fon, and is in good hopes of another living in Suffolk, that country of tranquillity, where he will then burrow

himfelf

himſelf in a wife and be happy.   Good-natured obliging Millar is as uſual.

Though the Doctor * increaſes in his buſineſs,

* Doctor Armſtrong.——Armſtrong was a worthy man, a good phyſician, and perhaps one of the beſt ſcientific didactic poets in the world, as appears from his poem on the Art of preſerving Health. Thomſon has deſcribed his abſent moods in the Caſtle of Indolence, in the tenth ſtanza:

" With him was ſometimes join'd in ſilent walk,
" (Profoundly ſilent, for they never ſpoke)
" One ſhyer ſtill, who quite deteſted talk ;
" Oft ſtung by ſpleen, at once away he broke,
" To groves of pine, and broad o'erſhadowing oak :
" There, inly thrill'd, he wander'd all alone,
" And on himſelf his penſive fury woke ;
" He never utter'd word, ſave when firſt ſhone
" The glittering ſtar of eve——Thank Heaven ! the day
    is done."

When the good Doctor was with the Britiſh army

bufineſs, he does not decreaſe in ſpleen ;
but there is a certain kind of ſpleen, that
is both humane and agreeable, like Jacques
in the play.   I ſometimes have a touch of
it.—But I muſt break off this chat with
you about our friends, which, were I to
indulge it, would be endleſs—As for politics—we are I believe upon the brink of
a peace.   The French at preſent, are va-
pouring in the ſiege of Maeſtricht, at the
ſame time they are mortally ſick in their
marine, and through all the vitals of
France.   It is a pity we cannot continue
the war a little longer, and put their ago-
niſing trade quite to death.   This ſiege,

in Flanders, as ſurgeon or phyſician, he was taken
priſoner one day, taking what he called a ſtroll beyond the lines.   I cannot but remember with high
pleaſure that worthy character.   He died September
30, 1779, much regretted by all who had the pleaſure of his acquaintance.

T

I take

I take it, they mean as their laſt flouriſh in the war.—May your health, which never failed you yet, ſtill continue, till you have ſcraped together enough to return home, and live in ſome ſnug corner, as happy as the Corycius Senex, in Virgil's fourth Georgic, whom I recommend both to you and myſelf as a perfect model of the trueſt happy life. Believe me to be ever moſt ſincerely, and affectionately,

Yours, &c.

JAMES THOMSON.

ODE

ODE ON THE DEATH OF THOMSON.

BY MR. COLLINS.

The Scene on the Thames near Richmond.

I.

IN yonder grave a Druid lies,
　　Where flowly winds the ftealing wave;
The year's beft fweets fhall duteous rife
　　To deck its poet's fylvan grave.

II.

In yon deep bed of whifp'ring reeds
　　His airy harp* fhall now be laid,
That he, whofe heart in forrow bleeds,
　　May love thro' life the foothing fhade.

III.

Then maids and youths fhall linger here,
　　And while its founds at diftance fwell,
Shall fadly feem in pity's ear
　　To hear the woodland pilgrim's knell.

---

* The Æolian harp.

IV. Re-

IV.

Remembrance oft fhall haunt the fhore
    When Thames in fummer wreaths is dreft,
And oft fufpend the dafhing oar,
    To bid his gentle fpirit reft !

V.

And oft, as eafe and health retire
    To breezy lawn, or foreft deep,
The friend fhall view yon whitening * fpire,
    And 'mid the varied landfcape weep.

VI.

But thou, who own'ft that earthy bed,
    Ah ! what will every dirge avail ;
Or tears, which love and pity fhed,
    That mourn beneath the gliding fail !

VII.

Yet lives there one, whofe heedlefs eye
    Shall fcorn thy pale fhrine glimm'ring near ?

---

* Richmond church, where Thomfon lies buried in the north-weft corner of it, below the chriftening pew, without a tablet or memorial to fay—Here Thomfon lies.

With

With him, fweet bard, may fancy die,
  And joy defert the blooming year.

VIII.

But thou, lorn ftream, whofe fullen tide
  No fedge-crown'd fifters now attend,
Now waft me from the green hill's fide,
  Whofe cold turf hides the buried friend !

IX.

And fee, the fairy valleys fade,
  Dun night has veil'd the folemn view :
Yet once again, dear parted fhade,
  Meek nature's child, again adieu !

X.

The genial meads affign'd to blefs
  Thy life, fhall mourn thy early doom ;
Their hinds and fhepherd-girls fhall drefs
  With fimple hands thy rural tomb.

XI.

Long, long, thy ftone and pointed clay
  Shall melt the mufing Briton's eyes :
O ! vales, and wild woods, fhall he fay,
  In yonder grave your Druid lies.

T 3   THE

THE REVEREND MR. WILLIAM THOMSON's

(Sometime of Queen's College, Oxford)

ADDRESS TO THE SHADE OF THOMSON*.

HAIL, nature's poet ! whom she taught alone
To sing her works in numbers like her own :
Sweet as the thrush that warbles in the dale,
And soft as Philomela's tender tale.
She lent her pencil too, of wondrous pow'r,
To catch the rainbow, and to paint the flow'r
Of many mingling hues ; then smiling said
(But first with laurel crown'd her fav'rite's head),
" These beauteous children, tho' so fair they shine,
" Fade in *my* seasons—let them live in *thine* :"
And live they shall, the charm of ev'ry eye,
Till nature sickens, and the seasons die.

---

* These beautiful and applicable lines were pronounced
by Lord Buchan, on Ednam Hill, on the 22d of September 1791, when he crowned the first edition of the Seasons
with a wreath of bays.

Anniverfary of Thomfon's Birth-day, 1790.

THE Earl of Buchan, defirous of promoting a fubfcription for erecting a monument to the memory of Thomfon on Ednam Hill, circulated letters to a confiderable number of gentlemen of Berwick and Roxburghfhires, in the beginning of September, inviting them to celebrate the 22d of September at a Mrs. Spinks's, in Ednam village, where Sir James Pringle, Sir Alexander Don, Dr. Bell, of Coldftream, the poet's fifter's fon, and a dozen more gentlemen accordingly met, and paffed the evening with attick feftivity and good humour, the Earl of Buchan fitting as præfes in the chair whereon the poet fat when he compofed his Caftle of Indolence.   This chair became the property of Dr. Arm-

T 4

ftrong,

ftrong, who had it from Sir Andrew Mitchel, who left it to Mr. Elliot, and by him it was obligingly fent to accommodate the prefident member of this fociety, upon this occafion.

The gentlemen who affembled on this day refolved to meet annually on its anniverfary*, and to open a fubfcription for erecting

---

* It is remarkable that Mrs. Mary Thomfon, fifter of the poet, and mother of Mr. Craig, architect, was buried on this day; and that while Lord Buchan was on Ednam Hill to celebrate the anniverfary, the fon was dropping the laft cord into the grave of Thomfon's fifter. The fame day likewife, though without previous concert, the fociety, at Ednam, called the Knights of the Cape, met in their hall at Ednam, to celebrate the birth-day of the bard. Mr. Woods, the comedian, recited a handfome occafional poem of his own compofition in honour of the day. On the toaft being

erecting a monument on Ednam Hill, requesting the Earl of Buchan to apply to the curators of Mr. Cuthbert, of Ednam, the proprietor of Ednam, a minor, for a grant of the fpot neceffary for the building and its appurtenances.

In returning from this meeting the Earl of Buchan's carriage, in which he was

being given to the memory of Thomfon, Mr. Woods recited, from a poem of Dr. Langhorne's, the conteft of the Seafons, who are reprefented as appealing to Thomfon to decide on their refpective merits. At proper intervals he afterwards delivered passages from the four Seafons of the author, each being followed by fongs applicable to the refpective fubjects, by other members of the fociety. Mr. Woods then recited a number of paffages, felected by him from Thomfon's Poem of Liberty; after which Rule Britannia was fung by the whole company on their legs, with which this attick entertainment concluded.

accom-

accompanied by Sir Alexander Don, and Mr. Thomas Potts, writer at Kelfo, was overturned by a reftive horfe on the approach to Ednam Bridge, but without any worfe confequences than the breaking of the machine. In the fucceeding year, Lord Buchan obtained a conceffion of promife from the curators of Mr. Cuthbert, for a grant of the fpot neceffary for erecting a monument on the fummit of Ednam Hill, and he circulated letters to the gentlemen who had attended the former anniverfary, and to many other perfons of diftinction and learning in Scotland; to Meffrs. Hayley, Mafon, Beattie, and Burns. But very few gentlemen paid any attention to the notification; a caft from the buft of the poet in Weftminfter Abbey, which had been generoufly tranfmitted by Mr. Coutts, banker at London, to be

crowned

crowned with a wreath of bays, was broken in a midnight frolick during the race week on the 16th of September; and the Earl of Buchan contented himself with impofing a wreath of laurel, dreffed by Mr. Robert Craig, architect, the poet's fifter's fon, on a copy of the Seafons, printed 1730, in 4to, being the firft complete edition prefented by the poet to his father, addreffing the fhade of the poet, in the beautiful apoftrophe compofed for a blank leaf of the Seafons by the Rev. Mr. William Thomfon, of Queen's College, Oxon, a copy of which is here publifhed. I fhall now fubmit to the perufal of the reader, Mr. Burns * the Airfhire

bard's

* Robert Burns, of Airfhire, a farmer's fon, remarkable for a genuine vein of Doric poetry, and for his fuperior abilities and good fenfe, which have ena-

bled

bard's apology for not attending the meeting, and his addrefs to the fhade of Thomfon.

———

My Lord,

LANGUAGE finks under the ardour of my feelings, when I would thank your Lordfhip for the honour, the very great honour, you have done me, in inviting me to the coronation of the buft of Thomfon.

bled him to efcape the fhipwreck of the fons of Apollo, by continuing his profeffion of a farmer.

Mr. Millar, of Dalfwinton, a gentleman well known by his great genius in mechanics, and his eminence as a banker, generoufly gave the young poet a comfortable and agreeable farm at Ellifland, near Dumfries, where he wooes his ruftic mufe in eafe with that native dignity which muft ever arife from fuperior tafte. "Spernit humum fugiente " penna."

—In

—In my firſt enthuſiaſm, on reading the card you did me the honour to write to me, I overlooked every obſtacle, and determined to go; but I fear it will not be in my power.—A week or two in the very middle of my harveſt, is what I much doubt I dare not venture on.—I once already made a pilgrimage *up* the whole courſe of the Tweed, and fondly would I take the ſame delightful journey *down* the windings of that charming ſtream.

Your Lordſhip hints at an ode for the occaſion: but who would write after, Collins? I read over his verſes to the memory of Thomſon, and deſpaired. I attempted three or four ſtanzas in the way of addreſs to the ſhade of the bard, on crowning his buſt.—I trouble your Lordſhip with the incloſed copy of them, which

I am

I am afraid will be but too convincing a proof how unequal I am to the tafk you would obligingly affign me.——However, it affords me an opportunity of approaching your Lordfhip, and declaring how fincerely I have the honour to be,

　　My Lord,

　　　　Your Lordfhip's highly obliged,

　　　　　　And moft devoted humble fervant,

　　　　　　　　ROBERT BURNS.

Ellifland, near Dumfries,
　　29th Auguft, 1791.

ADDRESS TO THE SHADE OF THOMSON,

On crowning his Buſt with a Wreath of Bays.

I.

WHILE virgin Spring, by Eden's flood,
  Unfolds her tender mantle green;
Or pranks the fod in frolic mood,
  Or tunes Eolian ſtrains between;

II.

While Summer with a matron grace
  Retreats to Dryburgh's cooling ſhade,
Yet oft delighted ſtops to trace
  The progreſs of the ſpiky blade;

III.

While Autumn, benefactor kind,
  By Tweed erects her aged head,
And fees, with felf-approving mind,
  Each creature on her bounty fed;

IV.

While maniac Winter rages o'er
  The hills whence claſſic Yarrow flows,

Rouſing

Rousing the turbid torrent's roar,
    Or sweeping wild a waste of snows;

V.

So long, sweet poet of the year,
    Shall bloom that wreath thou well hast won.
While Scotia with exulting tear
    Proclaims that Thomson was her son.

THE EARL OF BUCHAN'S INVITATION TO SIR JOHN
SINCLAIR, OF ULBSTER, TO BE PRESENT
AT THE FESTIVAL OF THOMSON.   1791.

SINCLAIR! thou phœnix of the frozen Thule!
O shape thy course to Tweda's lovely stream,
Whose lucid, sparkling, gently flowing course
Winds like Ilissus through a land of song:
Not as of old, when, like the Theban twins,
Her rival children tore each other's breasts,
And stained her silver wave with kindred blood:
But proudly glittering through a happy land,
The yellow harvests bend along her fields;
The golden orchards glow with blushing fruits;
Green are her pastoral banks, white are her flocks,
That safely stray where barb'rous Edward raged;
And where the din of clashing arms was heard
We hear the carols of the happy swains,
Free as their lords, and with the purring looms,
Hark, hark, the weaver's merry roundelay!
The charming song of Scotland's better day:
'Tis liberty, sweet liberty alone
Can give a lustre to the northern sun.
" Come when the Virgin gives the beauteous days,

U

" And

" And Libra weighs in equal fcales the year;"

Come, and to Thomfon's gentle fhade repair,

And pour libations to his virtuous mufe,

Where firft he drew the flame of vital air,

" Where firft his feet did prefs the virgin fnow,

" And where he tuned his charming Doric reed."

Perhaps where Thomfon fired the foul of fong,

Some voice may whifper in Æolian ftrains

To him who, wand'ring near his parent ftream,

Shall o'er the placid blue profound of air

Receive the genius of his paffing fhade.

Come then, my Sinclair, leave empiric Pitt,

And raging Burke, and all the hodge-podge fry

Of Tory Whigs, and whiggifh Tory knaves,

And bathe thy genius in thy country's fame :

Let Burke write pamphlets, and let Pitt declaim ;

Let us feek honour in our country's weal.

Eulogy

Eulogy of Thomson, the Poet, delivered by the Earl of Buchan, on Ednam Hill, when he crowned the firſt edition of the Seaſons with a wreath of bays, on the 22d of September, 1791.

GENTLEMEN,

IT has been the cuſtom of that great and truly to be reſpected nation of the French, to pronounce, at the meetings of men of genius, learning, and taſte, the praiſes of the illuſtrious dead; and this cuſtom has been adopted by other countries, as, emerging from barbarity, they became gradually ſenſible of the infinite ſuperiority of men imbued with ſcience, learning, and taſte, over the ignorant creatures of imperial power.

U 2

They

They faw, and deplored, the rude inftitutions of their favage anceftors on the
page of hiftory, inftitutions which covered
men' with honours, and beftrung them
with ribbands, according to the guft and
prejudice of illiterate princes, and left the
real benefactors and ornaments of fociety
to languifh or to pafs unnoticed in obfcurity. Fortunately born as we have
been in the age of a Frederick the Great,
and of a Wafhington, all men . poffeffed
of any tafte or feeling (and may I add)
of common fenfe, have rejoiced, and do
now rejoice, to behold the dignity of human nature beginning to appear amidft
the ruins of Gothic fuperftition and
tyranny, and the immortal Pruffia, ftanding like a herald in the proceffion of ages,
to mark the beginning of that order of.

men

men who are to banifh from the earth
the filly delufions of worthlefs prieftcraft, and the monftrous prerogatives of
defpotic authority.

I think myfelf happy to have this day
the tafk affigned to me of endeavouring
to do juftice to the memory of Thomfon,
which has been prophanely touched by
the rude hands of the pedantic Samuel
Johnfon, whofe fame and reputation in-
dicates the decline of tafte in a country
that, after having produced an Alfred, a
Wallace, a Bacon, a Napier, a Newton,
a Buchanan, a Milton, a Hampden,
a Fletcher, and a Thomfon, can fubmit.
to be bullied under the rod of a fchool-
mafter, or to be led by the ftrings of
the fatchel of a petulant fchool-boy?

Scotland, Gentlemen, though now full

                    of

of men who are above fervile compliance
with the power of the day, was, in the
days of Thomfon, a nation of proud and
poor nobles and difpirited vaffals. Except
Belhaven and Fletcher, whom he hardly
faw, and Argyll, Stair, Marchmont, and
other free fpirits, whom delicacy forbids
me to mention, there were few in the
kingdom who could encourage the poet
to rife above the mediocrity of a fettered
ftudent of divinity, or to imbue his mind
with that noble fentiment of independence
by which his life and his writings are
characterifed and diftinguifhed.   In the
family of Jervifwood, to which he was
introduced by the kindred of his mother,
he received the earlieft attentions; and
fome verfes of his addreffed to one of
that family, for the ufe of fome books,

are,

are, I believe, still preserved as a specimen of his infantine genius.

That the lady indiscreetly alluded to in the Life of Thomson, should have encouraged him to try his fortune in London, is highly probable; but that she should have deserted him afterwards agrees not with the nature of a spontaneous patronage; for nothing is more natural to patrons than the desire of seeing due attention paid to their recommendations, and following out the objects of their protection to the attainment of honour, that shall reflect upon themselves.

The trifling story about his losing his bundle on his way from Wapping to Mallet's house in London, and the want of his shoes, is in the odour of that vulgar malevolence, which gives a *race* to the works of the *savage* biographer.

U 4

The

The only occasion, when I had the mischance to meet Johnson, was at old Strahan's (the translator of the six first books of the Æneid), in Suffolk Street, where I found him and Mallet cobling these books for publication; and there I remember to have heard them repeating this story with glee, after having cut down Dryden, Gawin, Douglas, Trapp, and the other predecessors of poor Strahan, in the translation of the Æneid.

Such are the annals of critics, and poetasters, and with this blacking let them be handed down to posterity, with the shoes of the bard of Ednam.

We are much indebted to Aaron Hill for his kindness to Thomson, and his handsome lines in compliment to Scotland, now in every mouth: no more poetry and prophecy, but matter of fact!

How

How different an Aaron Hill, a Thomas Pennant, and a Thomas Newte, from a Samuel Johnson ! ✗

Why, says Johnson, are the dedications to Winter, and the other Seasons, contrary to custom, left out in Thomson's collected works? I will tell you, shade of Johnson. *Because little men* disappear when great men take their proper station.

The Countess of Hertford, says Johnson, used to invite every summer some poet to hear her verses; and Thomson, who was called for that purpose, took more delight in carousing with Lord Hertford and his friends, than in assisting her Ladyship's poetical operations, who therefore never gave the poet another summons.

That no earl or countess ever gave

Johnson

Johnfon an invitation to the country
can excite no wonder, nor that Thomfon's
genius and independant fpirit fhould lead
him to prefer wit and the focial board
of an accomplifhed family, to the manufacture of courtly verfes, for a verfe-fick
countefs.

Lord Chatham, Lord Temple, Lord
Lyttelton, Sir Andrew Mitchel, Dr.
Armftrong, Mr. Gray, of Richmond-
Hill, and the oily man of God, I
have often had the pleafure to hear on
the fubject of Thomfon. All of them
agreed in the teftimony of his being a
gentleman at all points, and a gentleman
by God, as well as a poet by nature, far
above the degree of our modern poets,
that are infufed into the houfe of bards,
in imitation of our modern fyftem of
peerage.

Of

Of Johnson's criticism on the Poem of Thomson, entitled Liberty, I shall say nothing; but I will take the liberty to say that Britain knows nothing of the liberty that Thomson celebrates!

Thomson

Thomſon to the Siſter of his Amanda, at Bath.

Kew Lane, Nov. 27, 1742.

MADAM,

GIVE me leave to ſay that, among all your friends, nobody longs more ardently after the full eſtabliſhment of your health than I do : firſt, and foremoſt, upon your own perſonal account ; and ſecondly, from more ſelfiſh motives, that you may ſoon return to ſupply to us the want of the ſun by your company. You may, perhaps, think this compliment a little highſtrained ; whereas, upon the faith of a melancholy man, and as I hope to laugh again, I would, for three or four hours of your company, give three or four months of ſuch days as theſe. But at the

fame

same time I must be so bold as to add, that though it be downright deep November, and you, Miss Berry, and Miss Young absent, none of us will push the compliment so far as to verify the French author's observation, who begins his book thus—It was in the month of November, when Englishmen hang and drown themselves—And yet, I am dismal enough, sometimes, nay—would you believe it?— as it were, vapoured. Do, dear Mrs. Robertson, make haste to be well.

Sorely do I grieve not to have been one of your 'squires that day you set out; for, besides the serious pleasure of attending you and your companions, I hear very diverting accounts of the journey, particularly of David's navigation on horseback; how it blew a hard gale of riding with him, driving him now a great

way

way on one fide, then, helm-a-lee, on
the other; how he had almoft committed
piracy on the highway; and how he was
next morning, while afleep, deferted by
the fhip's crew, and left among the fa-
vages. I am furthermore informed that,
being thereunto moved by the inftigation
of a galled backfide, and not having the
fear of the ladies before his eyes, he was
guilty of high treafon againft their fovereign beauty, by uttering certain bafe,
fcandalous, and traiterous words, for the
which he muft in due time undergo his
trial; George Scot *, judge; James Robertfon †, attorney general; and William

* George Lewis Scot, afterwards fub-preceptor
to the king, and one of the commiffioners of ex-
cife.

† Mr. Robertfon, furgeon to the houfehold at
Kew.

Paterfon

Paterſon *, foreman of the jury. But, by their mutual accuſations, I find there is a heavy charge againſt them all.

To think of leaving, nay, for ſome time actually to have left, diſtreſſed ladies under their protection, to travel in the dark through infamous places, through Maidenhead Thicket, where ſo many robberies had been committed the very day before, is ſuch a ſtain upon all chivalry, as their return cannot entirely wipe off. They were, indeed, upon the brink of perdition; for had they not returned, their ſwords muſt have been broken over their heads, their arms reverſed, and the ban of all gallantry publiſhed againſt them. Nobody would have drunk, no-

* Paterſon, formerly mentioned, who was then a clerk in a compting houſe, afterwards Thomſon's deputy as ſurveyor of the Leeward Iſlands.

5   body

body would have toafted with them, and nothing but making two or three campaigns in the fervice of that heroic lady, the Queen of Hungàry, could have reftored them to any degree of honour.

I hope the ladies have at laft got their clothes. To be at Bath, yet debarred from the rooms, muft have been a cruel fituation to fuch as knew lefs how to converfe with, and enjoy themfelves— the very fituation of Tantalus!. up to the lip in diverfions, without being able to catch a drop of them.—And yet, notwithftanding all thefe diverfions, I do, from my foul, moft fincerely pity you, to be fo long doomed to a place fo delightfully tirefome. Delightfully, did I fay ? No; it is merely a fcene of waking dreams, where nothing but the phantoms of pleafure fly about, without any fub-

ftance

ftance or reality. What a round of filly amufements, what a giddy circle of *nothing* do thefe children of a larger fize run every day! Nor does it only give a gay vertigo to the head, it has equally a bad influence on the heart. When the head is full of nothing but drefs, and fcandal, and dice, and cards, and rowly powly, can the heart be fenfible to thofe fine emotions, thofe tender, humane, generous paffions that form the foul of all virtue and happinefs! Ah! then, ye lovers, never think to make any impreffion on the hearts of the diffipated fair. So could I proceed in my tedious homily; but I afk pardon for railing at a place you are obliged to be at, and which I hope will reftore you to perfect health. Yes, that reconciles me to it again; and if my letter was not already too long, I would make its panegyric.

X

May

May I flatter myſelf with the hopes of hearing from you? If you ſend me but your three names, and above them—" We are well," I ſhall be glad even of that.— Madam, I am ſorry to acquaint you, that your huſband, once famous for hoſpitality, has loſt it all ſince you left this place. Pray be ſo good as to lay your commands upon him, to treat us ſome night or other with a bowl of punch, that we may drink your healths.   My beſt compliments, my moſt hearty reſpects, my—in ſhort, all the good wiſhes my heart can form, attend you all!   Believe me to be,

  With the utmoſt reſpect,

   Madam,

    Your, and Miſs Young's,

    And Miſs Berry's,

     Devoted humble ſervant,

     JAMES THOMSON.

Humorous

Humorous Epiſtle to a Friend, on his Travels.

December 7, 1742.

TRUSTY AND WELL-BELOVED DOG,

HEARING you are gone abroad to ſee the world, as they call it, I cannot forbear, upon this occaſion, tranſmitting you a few thoughts.

It may ſeem preſumption in me to pretend to give you any inſtruction; but you muſt know, that I am a dog of conſiderable experience. Indeed I have not improved ſo much as I might have done, by my juſtly deſerved misfortunes: the caſe very often of my betters.

However, a little I have learned; and ſometimes, while I ſeemed to lie aſleep before the fire, I have overheard the converſation of your travellers.

In

In the firft place, I will not fuppofe that you are gone abroad an illiterate cub, juft efcaped from the lafh of your keeper, and running wild about the world like a dog who has loft his mafter, utterly unacquainted with the proper knowledge, manners, and converfation of dogs.

Thefe are the public jefts of every country through which they run poft, and frequently they are avoided as if they were mad dogs. None will converfe with them but thofe who fhear, fometimes even fkin them, and often they return home like a dog who has loft his tail. In fhort, thefe travelling puppies do nothing elfe but run after foreign bitches, learn to dance, cut capers, play tricks, and admire your fine outlandifh howling: though in my opinion, our vigorous, deep-mouthed Britifh note is better mufic.

.If a timely ſtop is not put to this, the genuine breed of our ancient ſturdy dogs will, by degrees, dwindle and degenerate into dull Dutch maſtiffs, effeminate Italian lapdogs, or tawdry, impertinent French harlequins. All our once noble-throated guardians of the houſe and fold will be ſucceeded by a mean courtly race, that ſnarl at honeſt men, flatter rogues, proudly wear badges of ſlavery, ribbands, collars, &c. and fetch and carry ſticks at the lion's court. By the bye, my dear Marquis, this fetching and carrying of ſticks is a diverſion you are too much addicted to, and, though a diverſion, unbecoming a true independent country dog. There is an-other dog-vice, that greatly prevails among the hungry whelps at court; but your gut is too well ſtuffed to fall into that. What I mean is, patting, pawing, ſolicit-

ing,

ing, teafing, fnapping the morfel out of one another's mouths, being bitterly envious, and infatiably ravenous, nay, fometimes filching when they fafely may. Of this vice I have an inftance continually before my eyes, in that wretched animal Scrub, whofe genius is quite mifplaced here in the country. He has, befides, fuch an admirable talent at fcratching at a door, as might well recommend him to the office of a court-waiter—A word in your ear—I wifh a certain two-legged friend of 'mine had a little of his affiduity. Thefe canine courtiers are alfo extremely given to bark at merit and virtue, if illclad and poor: they have likewife a nice difcernment, with regard to thofe whom their mafter diftinguifhes: to fuch you fhall fee them go up immediately, and fawning in the moft abject . manner—

baifer

baiſer leur cul. For me, it is always a maxim with me,

> To honour humble worth, and, ſcorning ſtate,
> Piſs on the proud inhoſpitable gate.

For which reaſon I go ſcattering my water every where about Richmond. And now that I am upon this topic, I muſt cite you two lines of a letter from Bounce (of celebrated memory), to Fop, a dog in the country to a dog at court. She is giving an account of her generous offspring, among which ſhe mentions two, far above the vice I now cenſure:

> One uſhers friends to Bathurſt's door,
> One fawns at Oxford's on the poor!

Charming dogs! I have little more to ſay; but only, conſidering the great mart of ſcandal you are at, to warn you againſt flattering thoſe you converſe with, and,

X 4

the

the moment they turn to go away, back-
biting them—a vice with which the dogs
of old ladies are much infected: and you
muft have been moft furioufly affected
with it here at Richmond, had you not
happened into a good family; therefore
I might have fpared this caution.—One
thing I had almoft forgot. You have a
bafe cuftom, when you chance upon a
certain fragrant exuvium, of perfuming
your carcafe with it. Fye! fye! leave
that nafty cuftom to your little, foppifh,
crop-eared dogs, who do it to conceal
their own ftink.

My letter, I fear, grows tedious. I will
detain you from your flumbers no longer,
but conclude by wifhing that the waters
and exercife may bring down your fat
fides, and that you may return a genteel
accomplifhed dog. Pray lick for me, you

happy

happy dog you, the hands of the fair ladies you have the honour to attend. I remember to have had that happiness once, when one, who fhall be namelefs, looked with an envious eye upon me.

Farewell, my dear Marquis. Return, I beg it of you, foon to Richmond; when I will treat you with fome choice frag-ments, a marrow-bone which I will crack for you myfelf, and a deffert of high-toafted cheefe. I am, without farther ceremony, yours fincerely,

B U F F.

Mi Dewti too Marki. X Scrub's mark.

Letter to Mrs. R. the Sifter of Amanda.

Chriftmas Day, 1742.

MADAM,

I BELIEVE I am in love with fome one or all of you; for though you will not

favour

3

favour me with the scrap of a pen, yet I cannot forbear writing to you again. Is it not however barbarous, not to send me a few soft characters, one pretty name to cheer my eyes withal? How easily some people might make others happy if they would! But it is no small comfort to me, since you will not write, that I shall soon have the pleasure of being in your company. And then, though I were downright picqued, I shall forget it all in a moment.

I cannot help telling you of a very pleasing scene I lately saw.————In the middle of a green field there stands a peaceful lowly habitation; into which having entered, I beheld innocence, sweet innocence, asleep. Your heart would have yearned, your eyes perhaps overflowed with tears of joy, to see how charming

he

he looked; like a young cherub dropped from Heaven, if they be so happy as to have young cherubs there.

When awaked, it is not to be imagined with what complacency and ease, what soft serenity altogether unmixed with the least cloud, he opened his eyes. Dancing with joy in his nurse's arms, his eyes not only smiled, but laughed— which put me in mind of a certain near relation of his, whom I need not name.

What delights thee so, thou lovely babe? art thou thinking of thy mother's recovery? does some kind power imprefs upon thee a presage of thy future happiness under her tender care?—I took the liberty to touch him with unhallowed lips, which restored me to the good opinion of the nurse, who had neither forgot nor forgiven my having slighted that favour

once.

once. While thus I gazed with sincere and virtuous satisfaction, I could most pathetically have addressed the gay wretches of the age, the joyless inmates of Bachelor's Hall *, and was ready to repeat Milton's divine Hymn on Marriage:

> Hail, wedded Love! mysterious law, true source
> Of human offspring, sole propriety
> In Paradise of all things common else!
> By thee adulterous lust was driven from men
> Among the bestial herds to range; by thee,
> Founded in reason, loyal, just and pure,
> Relations dear, and all the charities
> Of father, son, and brother, first were known.
> Far be it, &c.

Now that I have been transcribing

---

* Bachelor's Hall, a house on Richmond Hill; so called, from being occupied during the summer season by a society of gentlemen from London.

some

some lines of poëtry, I think I once engaged myself while walking in Kew-lane
to write two or three songs. The following is one of them, which I have stolen
from the Song of Solomon; from that
beautiful expression of Love, " Turn
away thine eyes from me, for they have
overcome me."

I.

O THOU, whose tender serious eyes
Expressive speak the mind I love;
The gentle azure of the skies,
The pensive shadows of the grove:

II.

O mix their beauteous beams with mine,
And let us interchange our hearts;
Let all their sweetness on me shine,
Pour'd thro' my soul be all their darts.

III.

Ah! 'tis too much! I cannot bear
At once so soft, so keen, a ray:

In pity, then, my lovely fair,
O turn thefe killing eyes away!

IV.

But what avails it to conceal
One charm, where nought but charms we fee?
Their luftre then again reveal,
And let me, Myra, die of thee.

My beft refpects attend Mifs Young and Mifs Berry, who I hope are heartily tired of Bath, and will leave it without the leaft regret, whomfoever they leave pining behind them. I wifh you all a much happier and merrier Chriftmas than we can have without you. But in amends you will bring us along with you a gay and happy new year. Believe me to be, with the greateft refpect, and the heartieft good wifhes that all health and happinefs may ever attend you,

Madam,

Your moft obedient,

Humble fervant,

JAMES THOMSON.

Verses addressed to Miss Young.

AH urge too late! from beauty's bondage free,
Why did I truft my liberty with thee?
And thou, why didft thou, with inhuman art,
If not refolv'd to take, feduce my heart?
Yes, yes, you faid (for lovers eyes fpeak true);
You muft have feen how faft my paffion grew:
And when your glances chanc'd on me to fhine,
How my fond foul ecftatic fprung to thine!
　　But mark me, fair-one, what I now declare
Thy deep attention claims, and ferious care:
It is no common paffion fires my breaft,
I muft be wretched, or I muft be bleft!
My woes all other remedy deny;
Or, pitying, give me hope, or bid me die!

To

TO MISS YOUNG*, WITH A PRESENT OF HIS SEASONS.

ACCEPT, loved nymph! this tribute due
To tender friendſhip, love, and you ;
But with it take what breath'd the whole,
O! take to thine the poet's ſoul.
If fancy here her pow'r diſplays,
And if a heart exalts theſe lays—
You faireſt in that fancy ſhine,
And all that heart is fondly thine.

———————————————————

* Some ſlight variations have been found in different copies which have been handed about in MS. This is from the original.

THE END.